1645 Olive Street, Baton Rouge, LA 70802

ISBN: 978-0-6151-3557-1

Lulu ID: 451824

This book is a work of fiction. Names, characters, places and
incidents are products of the author's imagination.
Information contained in this story is used fictitiously.
Any resemblance to actual events or locales or persons,
living or dead, is entirely coincidental.

Printed in the United States of America

That's The Way It Is

By

Sandra Lusk

Acknowledgements

All things are possible if you believe.
First and foremost I thank GOD.
For life and his gifts, each and everyone.

There are many special people in my
life who played significant
roles while writing this book.
I thank each and every one of you for
your part. I hope you enjoy
reading Maria's story.
I know many of you have been waiting
a long time for this. This is
truly a wonderful journey I am on and I am
happy to take you all along with me.

Affectionaly yours

Sandra

That's the way it is

While the song played, I fought back the tears. The song had my life in every lyric. He held my life captive for such a long time. How could someone have so much power over someone else? It is just too much to comprehend. "I will always remember the thought of you so tender" the words screamed out in my head. But you are gone- -- my mind was always letting the truth come in so clearly. No clouds, no rules, nothing but the truth. How do I let him go? How do I just walk away? My head tells me that I have to, but my heart is saying "I want you and I can't let go". "Not now, not like this". Mariah's songs are singing the words of my life right now, and I want to find him and tell him everything the songs I am listening to, they are the words meant for you alone. But………., he's gone, just gone. How do I start my life over without you? Where do I begin?

Along with the morning came the answers I had prayed for. I awakened to the sound of the music I had left playing during the night. Was yesterday a dream or did it all really happen. Did I really cut loose the ties that had me bound? Did I really put Kentrel out of my life for good this time? I keep telling myself that this is a good thing. I will get through this I know I will. But why does it hurt so badly? Why do I feel like I have lost my best friend in the whole world? I don't understand this. I know that I have done the right thing. As I moved about my morning along with the doom and gloom and letting my feelings rule my thoughts I had not thought about the time of day nor did I think about where I was suppose to be. I was over an hour late for church and it had never crossed my mind. The ringing of the phone broke my mood and I quickly picked it up. Sister? Yeah, I'm here. Why aren't you here? Has something happened to you, the voice said on the other end of the phone? What do you mean, where am I suppose to be? Church!! The voice answered from the phone. Oh God, I forgot. What time is it? I will be there in a few minutes. Sister, we were just worried about you cause you never miss a second Sunday morning service. Mama told me not to call you but I was worried, Angel said in an angelic voice. I will be there soon, okay sweetie? Ok sister, I will tell mama you are on your way. I jumped to my feet so fast that I couldn't catch my breath. I brushed my teeth and washed my face. I threw clothes everywhere in my bedroom. I finally got dressed and was out the door. I didn't have time to deal with Kentrel and what happened the day before. I had to clear my mind and get to church.

When I walked into the church almost an hour and a half late, I couldn't help but feel that all eyes were on me. I took a seat at the back of the church with hopes of not being more noticeable, especially by my mother. Angel noticed me coming in and she jumped to her feet and ran to greet me. Angel is such a sweet child and you can't help but love her. She is every parents dream baby and she is even more adorable as a five-year old. Pastor Martin is preparing for his sermon and everyone was preparing them selves for his message. As he began to speak, I felt that his eyes were piercing through to my soul. He started his passage saying that when we have trouble in our lives, we try to solve them all by ourselves. It is only when you don't get the results we are looking for that we turn to God. But do you know, that if you had looked him up in the first place, finding a solution would have been a bit easier. If you had of dialed the Almighty's number in the first place, you probably would not have gone through some of the hardships you've endured. Amen's were heard all around the church. Then I heard Pastor Martin say, "somebody is going through something right now, and if she would just reach out her hand to the Almighty, He can help you through it". A feeling welled up inside of me so bad that I just burst into tears. In my heart I wanted to say " Lord here I am, it's me, I am the one who needs you right now". "I am the one whose broken into so many pieces. I am the one who is so full of sin that I am too ashamed of myself. I am the one, Lord"! Before I knew it, the ushers were surrounding me with fans and water thinking that I was about to shout. Filled with even more humiliation I collected myself and continued to listen to what Pastor Martin had to say. Of course the nosy busy bodies of the church were just looking and wondering what was wrong with me. I could imagine them saying, what skeletons has she got hiding in her closet? If they only knew what I have done, I thought to myself. What I didn't know was that it was only the beginning of my humiliation. Adrenna is the cousin to Kentrel's best friend, Malik. And you know that men talk almost as much as women do. Adrenna had heard that the we had been seeing

each other and she got part of the dirt right
but not all of it. The part she got right was
more than enough hurt me and my family. So, she
just ad-libed the rest of it to get a good story
going. She had already started her rumors
before church service. Malik is the ultimate
"DOG" and you know how they travel in packs.
Well, Kentrel and Malik are both married men, at
least in the eyes of the law and the Almighty
God. Even if you are not together, you are
still married. I knew that this is not a
welcomed situation with my parents and that
there is no room for approval of my actions with
him in my family's life. So the issue of
Kentrel being married was never brought up. I
had not known that he was a married man until
long after I had fallen in love with him. We

had been involved for months when I actually found out.

I thought about things that had taken place over the last few weeks. Things had changed so much and I knew that Kentrel was up to some type of game. He was not available and I could not go anywhere with him. He always had some kind of excuse or Malik was riding with him. So, I finally realized that something was up. I reasoned with myself to have a talk with him. Of course the lies came and then came the I love you baby. But the truth was the only thing I wanted. Kentrel is a lover. He has the persuasive manner and the charm to match. He is accustomed to getting his way, even with me. But this particular day was different, I wanted answers and I wanted them now. Kentrel was sitting on the sofa as if nothing was wrong.

Where have you been Kentrel? Baby I told you, I
was out with the fellas. Why are you trippin?
I want to know what is going on. Don't lie to
me, Kentrel. It's Sheila isn't it? What makes
you think she is involved in any of this? So
you do admit that something is going on? Look
baby, I have some issues that I have to deal
with and I don't think that you need to get
involved. I am involved Kentrel and I should
know what is going on. I was hoping not to have
you involved in any of this, but I see you're
not gonna to let up. Okay, Sheila wants us to
get back together. I felt my heart stop
beating, when he said those words to me. I felt
like someone told me that apart of me had died.
Baby look, it's just a phase she is going
through. I have been spending a little time
with her. You know her mother died and she just

needed someone to-----. Maria, Maria, you listening to me? I was standing there as if I was someone else and I could not respond to him. When he put his hands on my shoulders and I looked up at him, I felt so angry. I knew that this had to end and that if I didn't do it now, it would go on forever. I finally made the lump in my throat disappear. You need to leave. What? You need to leave, I said again. Maria, listen to me. I know I can work this out. Just give me a little time. I want you to leave now, right now and don't come back. Why you trippin girl, you know I love you. Now come over here and let me show you how much. I turned away from him. You know I love you and I know that you love me too, he said. I walked over to the door and held it open. Now Kentrel. I was so in shock, that I didn't realize what I had done until I closed the door on him and walked away from it. In my head, I was saying it's over, and he is gone. But my heart was saying Oh God he is gone. My baby is gone; I have sent him away, now I'm alone. I must be out of my mind. I wanted to run to the door and call him back. Beg for his forgiveness, throw my arms around him and make love to him till the sun came up the next day. Instead, I cried all night. I would sleep a while and awake to hearing the sound of my own whimpers. Misery was my name now and until the hurt goes away, that's the way it is.

So, Pastor Martin was saying that things don't have to be the way they are. When you find yourself in a place that you don't want to be in, you can change it. He said some other things but I wasn't listening. I was thinking

of what I had to do to get my life back. I knew
that God had a plan for my life and the road I
was on was not a part of it. I needed to make a
change. I found myself hanging around after
church to talk to a few people. Girl what got
into you? I heard a voice say from behind me.
As I turned, I was staring into the face of
Adrenna and her mother. Good morning Mrs.
Simmons. Morning child, are you all right.
Yes, I am. Thank you for asking. Seems like
the Holy Spirit touched you this morning huh
child? Well, when you have to release something
to the Lord, you just have to let it go. Amen
to that Adrenna called out. You both have a
good morning I said as I eyed Adrenna and walked
away. Angel was jumping about, and wanting to
go home. Are you coming to our house sister?
Sure sweetie, I'm coming to your house. Yea,

can I ride with you? Sure, let's go see what mama has to say. Mama, Mama, Mama, sister is coming over, can I ride with her? Mrs. Dolace glanced over to Maria and as a mother knows her child she could see the hurt in her eyes. Yes Angel you can ride with your sister. Well how are you child, Mrs. Sara asked. I'm fine Mrs. Sara and how are you today? I'm doing fine. I'm still waiting on you to schedule some time to meet with our board for that finance class. I will see what I can do Mrs. Sara. Ok, I'll be waiting. You all ready to go, Mrs. Dolace asked. Yes mama, we're ready.

Angel talked non stop throughout the ride to her house. As I pulled up in the driveway, I could see my father working in the garage. Angel and I are both the light of his eyes. Mr. Dolace is so proud of his eldest daughter and

delighted with the youngest. How are you Daddy?
Just find my princess. How are you today? I
paused, and then I thought that if I said how I
really feel I would have to explain myself. I
finally said that I was fine. Let's go inside
Angel. See you later Daddy. I walked into the
house with Angel and I could smell the aroma of
a wonderful meal waiting for me. Church was
wonderful today wasn't it Mama? It sure was a
blessing, even the part you missed. Quietness
filled the room. You want to talk about it?
Not really Mama, I'm not ready yet. I could
always talk to my mother about anything, but not
this. She just would not understand the
reasoning behind a thing like this. I don't
understand it myself. The thoughts in my head
were interrupted by Mama's voice. Sugar, are
you sure you don't want to talk about it? Well,

it's Kentrel. Just as I started to tell Mama

about the breakup, Daddy walked in. What are my

favorite girls up to this morning? Oh nothing

special, I said as I gave my mother a look. I

know that my mother hates keeping secrets from

my father. But this time I didn't want to talk

to my father about this. Mr. Dolace could tell

that we were actually in the middle of something

so he politely made his way to another part of

the house. I could hear he and Angel singing

the words to Yes Jesus loves me. So, what's

this about Kentrel? Well we, I mean I decided

not to see him anymore. Is that what's got you

looking so broken up? What happen? Now it is

not like me to lie, but I found myself sprouting

out the lie of my life. He is seeing someone

else Mama. Well it's for the best. God will

heal your heart baby; you know the right thing

to do. Just put him in the Lords hands and it
will all work out. I know Mama. I was tired
and needed a change of pace so I decided to go
home. I really felt like being alone. After
saying my good byes to everyone I drove away
feeling alone and depressed.

CHAPTER TWO

This was my first adult relationship. I had never had a long-term relationship before. So this was so new to me. I had boyfriends before but never on this level. When I decided to move out of my parent's home and get a place of my own, I felt all grown up. Then I met Kentrel and growing up became real. After I turned the key to walk into my place, I heard Kentrel's voice calling my name. I was startled. I'm sorry; I didn't mean to scare you. Can I come in? I just want to talk to you? I don't know Kentrel; I'm not up for this right now. Please Maria. Just hear me out. I knew that he could sweet talk his way out of every argument we have ever had, mainly because he had not been out of my heart. We walked in and I turned to him and said, you have five minutes. Baby, don't write me off so fast. I told you I'm working things out. I am tired Kentrel and I'm not in the mood for your games. Kentrel walked up to me and touched my face with his hand. I moved away. He reached for my hand to hold me from putting distance between us. Please, he said in a tone that would just bring even the meanest woman to her knees. Tears fell from my eyes as I tried to hide them from him. Baby, don't cry, I never wanted to hurt you. I am trying to take care of so many people and I am messing everything up with you. I just want everything to be the way it was, cause I love you. I love you too I sobbed. I can't stand this situation Kentrel. You have to make this right. I can't go on like this anymore. I know baby, I know. I fell into his arms, while he held me tightly, not wanting

to let go. As the day faded into dust, we
walked around each other like we were afraid to
get in the others' space. Why are you keeping
your distance from me sweetness? I looked over
at him from the kitchen and shrugged my
shoulders. Kentrel got up and walked over to
me. I gently placed a cup into the cabinet and
reached for another dish. I could feel him
directly behind me. We were almost the same
height with him being a tad bit taller. Broad
shoulders and a chest that screams lay you head
on me.   Kentrel's size and shape would make
anyone looking at him would swear he played
football for some college team, but that was not
his thing. He loved to lift weights and that is
how he kept his great physique. Kentrel was my
first real love.   Everything I had learned
about making love was with him. I had grown use

to his touch and my body seemed to respond automatically to his. Kentrel gently caressed my arms with his masculine hands starting at my hands and made his way to the very tip-top of my shoulders. He placed small delicate kisses on my neck and cheeks. I decided to play hard to get and not be phased by him. You know I am really sorry that I hurt you and made you cry. I don't ever want to hurt you. He was really doing a job on me at this point. I thought, *how am I going to ignore all of this if he keeps talking to me?* I turned to say something to him and turned right into his lips. I knew then that it was impossible to resist him. He held my mouth captive to his for a while. This was definitely a new thing. Is he trying to prove something to me now? Looking at his size and stature, you would think that he didn't know how

to be gentle, but you would be wrong. He was
the gentlest creature I had ever met. I found
myself wrapped around him like a ribbon on a
Christmas present. We were so into each other
that I thought he would make love to me on the
kitchen floor. But, to my surprise, Kentrel
eased his lips away from mine and took me by the
hand leading me toward the other room. I
thought we were going to my bedroom but he went
to the sofa. Sit down sweetness, he said. I
want to talk to you. This was really strange.
Kentrel never gave up the opportunity to make
love to me before. Matter of fact he always
thought that this was his way of making up.
Maybe he is for real. Look sweetness, I have
really messed up and I don't want to continue to
do this. I want to be real with you. I don't
know where things will go from here. I want

everyone to be happy, but I am only one person. I want you in my life. I want us to continue to see each other. But I have to tell you that I have some responsibilities where my marriage is concerned. Sheila is pretty messed up and I don't know what to do about it. I don't want to lay all this on you but I feel it necessary to be straight with you. Right now I want you bad, but I can't do this with out being open with you. This can't be good for you either; I know what risk you are taking with your family by continuing a relationship with me. I kept quiet while he talked. Finally he stopped and waited for me to say something. I don't know what to say Kentrel. I just don't know what to say. He leaned over and kissed me gently on the lips. I know you need some time to think about this so, I'll leave so that you can do just that. Wait a minute, you tell me all of this and then you just leave me with it. Not to mention you have turned me on and now you leave me alone. How dare you do this to me? You are a jerk. Before I could say another word, he grabbed me and kissed me so deeply that I couldn't breathe. What do you want from me woman? I had never heard him talk like this before. I am trying to do the right thing he said, while they both gasped for another breath. I want you, Kentrel you know that I do. Maybe it was the intensity of our emotions that made us feel the way we did. We made love. Knowing that I wanted him after all that was said gave him such a rush. I lay in Kentrel's arms listening to his heartbeat wondering what are we going to do. With every breath he takes he feels confident that he has won her over again and things will continue as they are. He felt that if he could make her come down from her principles once again, he had it made. He would reconcile with his wife and still continue his every once in a while sleepovers with Maria. Malik was so right he thought to himself, this was too easy.

CHAPTER THREE

It's Monday morning and I was on cloud nine. I made the ride into work without problems this morning. Hello pretty lady, Jeffrey said as he does every weekday. Jeffrey is the security guard at the front desk. Good morning Jeffrey, how was your weekend? Just fine, just like you. Thank you and you have a good day I said as I stepped onto the elevator. He was leaning over his desk watching me as I stepped inside. Uh, Uh, Uh one-day pretty lady, one day he said. I would sometimes feel threatened by his overtures but I never let him know it. There was this time when I was on the elevator alone with him and he tried to come on to me. I made a point to have Kentrel pick me up the next day and he settled down on his approach towards me. However he still admires me and talks sweetly to me. Kentrel made the ladies drool the day he met me for lunch. I must admit he is stylish and with his bod he can't help it. When I returned from lunch, I was the envy of the office. Girl where did you find that man, Marla snickered? I want one just like him, Joycell announced.   Does he have a brother someone asked from across the room along with many others questions and comments? I causally smiled and waived them off. The one that got to me was the comment from Jeanette. She said "I know you think that you are all that and he looks like he could be all that, but did you know that two pretty people usually don't make it". Then she walked away flinging her hair. Others just looked at her and turned to say.

Don't worry about her she's just jealous cause she don't have a man. They all laughed.
Knowing what I had done to my life, I visited my folks less and less. When my Mama called to check up on me, I would always say I was busy and I couldn't come over. Guilt was eating me up inside. But the love I felt for Kentrel was pushing me on.

We talked very little about his marriage to Sheila. He felt it best and decided to keep that part of his life out of ours. But as fate would have it we were bound to cross paths eventually. Sheila and I had never seen each other, but we were aware of each other's presence in Kentrel's life. We were both being made fools of by the same man. Who would have guess that we had a mutual friend? Charlotte was a genuine people person and never met a stranger. She had tons of friends and knew everybody. While Charlotte and I were casual friends, Charlotte was a real good friend with Sheila's cousin DeAnn. Of course there had to be a BBQ and guess who was invited. DeAnn and Sheila are close cousins and she was at the BBQ. Introductions were being made as people arrived and Sheila was introduces as just Sheila. The nail was put in the coffin when Charlotte asked if Kentrel was coming too. Sheila replied no, Kent said he was hanging with Malik and some of the fellas today and that he was going to be gone all day. Whereas my plan was to spend the day with Kentrel but Charolette begged me to come to the BBQ. So I told Kentrel I would be home later on. I thought to myself, so this is Sheila. We were very similar in size and skin tone. The only difference was the hair. Sheila

had short hair that was styled very nice and I
wore my long locks curly and I would always pull
my hair up. We glanced at one another, and I
gave no indication that I knew who she was. The
evening passed perfectly without incident.
Later on that evening I finally got together
with Kentrel. I saw you wife this afternoon.
Sheila? You have another wife that I don't know
about? Where did you meet Sheila? At
Charlotte's BBQ. Uh, Uh Uh, well did you two
talk? You don't have to worry Kentrel; your
secret life is still in tact. I didn't talk to
your wife. Kentrel thought to himself, how
could this shit happen? This city is to damn
big for two people that don't know each other to
meet up. However, he played it off and played
his usual game of making me feel like I was the
only one for him. I am not up for this right

now Kentrel. Baby, I can make you feel better, just relax and let me do all the work. Kentrel, I said no! You are just a little stressed let me help you relax. Just feeling his hot breath on my neck was enough to move all the tension in my body straight out the door. I let myself submerge into his capable arms and let him do all the work. Kentrel was the master of our bedroom and he knew it. As we lay in bed together, exhausted and totally satisfied, I asked him if he really loved me. You know I do, Maria. Why would you ask me something like that? Do you love me enough to spend the rest of your life with me? You know if I could, baby I would. Right now I am giving you all that I have. But you will go home to Sheila when you leave here. Kentrel, you understand exactly what I am asking you, so don't play dumb. Why do you do this Maria? We just made love and you have to ruin everything with all of this. Why do you have to mess things up girl? Because I saw Sheila and she didn't look like anybody who was having a hard time. I am tire of being the other woman in your life, Kentrel. I just want someone for me, just for me. Can't you understand that Kentrel? I am doing the best that I can Maria. God, why does everyone want so much from me? I am just one man and I try to please everybody. It is amazing that he would just have a fit and I just let him turn the situation around and I end up petting him, forgetting that I was the injured party here. I am sorry Kentrel. I know you are doing the best that you can. I am just a little jealous that you are going home to her. I want you here with me. I need you too. I really am sorry, you forgive me? Baby I know that I leave you alone too much, he said. But I don't know what to do. Sure Sheila looks fine now, but I never told you that she tried to take her life and I just can't walk away from her right now. I don't want to be the reason she ends her life. I know you would not want that either. No, Kentrel I wouldn't be able to handle that. It'll all work out, you'll see sweetness. As he spoke the words to me he caressed my body in an attempt to ease me emotionally. Of course it worked as usual he was able to manipulate me with his touch.

CHAPTER FOUR

I would find myself just sitting at my desk and wondering about my life. Why am I doing this to myself? I know that there are some single men out there and I should be with one of them. But I love Kentrel. How can a man love two women the same way? I have been through this all before in my mind, but why can't I get past it? I had not even realized that the end of the day was so near and so was the week. Thursday evening and I have seen very little of Kentrel, I thought to myself on the ride home from work. I turned into my parking spot and took my time getting out of the car. I had always been an observant person but today I had so much on my mind that I was not paying attention to anything around me. Someone was moving into the apartment two doors down. There were several nice looking gentlemen coming in and out. I had my head down looking into the back seat of my car when a nice sounding gentleman said excuse me haven't I seen you somewhere before? I almost hit my head on the inside of the car when I tried to look up to see who was speaking to me. I'm sorry if I frightened you. My name is Harry. Harry Stonewell. I'm moving into the apartment over there. It's nice to meet you Harry. I'm Maria, Maria Dolace. Yeah, I thought I knew your face, he said. My mother attends Starlight Chapel with your mother. I saw you at church a few weeks ago. Flash backs came quickly across my mind about that Sunday morning service. Oh you were at service with your mother? Yes. You might know her by Mrs. Sara Whitney. She remarried after my father died. Oh yeah, Mrs. Sara, I know her. She and Mama are real good friends. I didn't know she had a son. I am her well-kept secret. I have been up state working. I see. The yelling of his friends for him to come on interrupted our conversation. Well, it was very nice meeting you Maria and I hope to see you soon. Maybe we could have dinner and get to know each other better. That would be really nice, I said. I'll stop by later this evening once I am settled then, he said. So I'll see you later, he said. I watched him as he walked away. My goodness, how God answers prayers. He is so fine. I don't think I could stand it. I over heard one of the guys say to him, "man you haven't spent one night in the place and you are picking up chicks". Man that is not a chick; she is a very good-looking female. The other guy said yeah and she is fine too. I want you all to stay away from her too, Harry said to them with authority and looking in my direction. I went into the apartment and headed straight for the shower. I thought I had the evening to myself when the doorbell rang. I had just about finished taking off my clothes, so I grabbed my robe and headed for the door. I peaked through and saw Malik's face. I opened the door to see what he wanted. Hi Malik, what are you doing here? I just wanted to come by and talk to you for a minute. Talk, about what? Do you mind if I come in? Well, I was about to take a shower. I can wait, he said as his eyes roamed my body. I think not. Come on girl, I just need to talk to you for a few minutes. Against my better judgment I let him in. I walked over to the sofa and sat down. What do

you want Malik? I talked to my boy the other
day and he told me that ya'll was chillin' on
your relationship. What? I said in a raised
voice as I stood up. He told me that he had to
take care of his wife. See, he said that he
decided to give you some space so that he could
handle up on his business with Sheila. Really?
Yeah, I figured that since ya'll was chillin',
that you and I could get to know each other a
little better. Get out! Get the hell out of my
house Malik. Baby, don't be so mean. I just
thought that we could spend some time together.
You are the sickest little dog I ever met in my
life Malik. Does Kentel know that he has such a
dog for a friend? Kentrel and I share thangs
and I don't see why you shouldn't be one of'em,
he said as he rubbed his chin, eyeing me up and
down. I see how you look at me when I be

hangin' with my boy. I know you want this, he said as he grabbed between his legs. You are sick Malik and I want you to get out of my house right now. He was walking towards me and I headed for the door. He grabbed me from behind by the hair and pulled me to the floor. I began fighting him, but he over powered my every move. During the tussle Malik pulled the robe from my body. He ripped my bra right off of my body and did the same to my panties. I kicked at him wildly, but to no end. Don't do this Malik I cried. You know you want this, so stop fightin', he said as he continued to press me to the floor. He held me down with the weight of his body. While he unzipped his pants, I pulled all the strength I could find and hit him across his face. That stopped him for a brief moment. He responded to my attempt to hurt him with a slap across my face. I felt like I was in a horrible dream. I knew that eventually I would wake and this nightmare would be over. But this nightmare was far from over. Malik raped me. He forced himself upon me like I was his property to do as he pleased. My screams went unheard as Malik plowed his tool in and out of my body repeatedly. The fight had left me and I had weakened beneath him. I could no longer feel the pain he was inflicting on my body. I felt numb. When he finally decided he was through with me, he whispered how much he enjoyed my company and that the next time he came over I should be a little more sociable. He stood up and pulled up his pants. Don't worry about Kentrel; he knows I'm here, he said as he headed for the door. I lay in the middle of the floor lifeless. I was afraid to move. I thought that if I moved he might come back. As I lay in the floor I began to feel the pain that Malik inflicted upon my body. I was wrenched with pain and disbelief of what had just happened to me. I cried as his words replayed over and over in my head. Malik didn't waste any more time with me. Just as he was opening the door, Harry was about to knock on it. Excuse me, Harry said. I am looking for Maria Dolace. Malik just brushed past him and kept walking. Harry heard a whimpering cry and pushed the door open to see my naked body lying in the middle of the floor, curled up like a baby. Oh my God. Maria! I was bruised and weakened from my fight and didn't answer him. He looked around for the phone and dialed 911. 911 what is your emergency? I need the police and an ambulance to Carmon Drive someone has been attacked. The Address is 3211. Your name sir, the operator asked? Harry Stonewell. Hurry, the guy just left, I ran into him when I got here. Sir, is the victim conscience? Yes. Sir, stay with the victim until the police arrives. I will he said, please hurry. Harry put the phone down and looked around for something to cover me up. He ran into the bedroom and grabbed the covers off the bed and wrapped them around me, picking me up and taking me over to the sofa. I cried as he carried me. I grabbed onto Harry as if he were my lifeline for the moment. That's it, hold on to me, he said. I've got you and I won't let anything else happen to you. You're going to be fine. However he didn't believe that because he was unsure of what had happened to me. I need to call your mother. I quickly shook my head no.

All right, I won't call your mother. Can I call someone for you? I nodded no again. Do you want me to say with you? Yes, just stay with me. My body was shaking as I spoke. Maria, did you know that guy? He is my boyfriends' best friend. Is he the one that attacked you? He raped me, I said as I began to cry again. Malik raped me. Harry held me closer to him and waited for the police to arrive. He finally heard the sirens approaching. He placed me on the sofa and went to the door to motion them in. When the Emergency Unit arrived he let them take care of me, while he talked to the police. He gave them as much information as he could and the rest would be up to me. We need to take her to Memorial one of the guys said to the officer. We will meet you there the officer told them. Harry looked around for my purse and keys and

locked my door and ran down to his truck, jumped
in and headed for the hospital. Once he reached
emergency, he found me by the crying coming from
the room. Sir, you can't go back there, a nurse
called out to him. Yes I can he said while
calling out my name. Once he located me, the
nurses let him stay with me. I felt safe when
Harry arrived, as if I had known him all of my
life. When the doctor came in, I jumped. I
understand that you were attacked. She was
raped Harry said. And who are you sir? I'm a
friend. Would you mind stepping outside for a
moment while I examine her? No! I screamed and
latched onto Harry's arm. All right Miss if you
want him to stay it's fine with me. Harry
didn't like the way the Doctor treated Maria.
He noted in his memory and planned to handle it
after she was treated. We are going to give you

a shot to calm you down a little and then the Doctor will examine you, ok the nurse said as she administered the medication. I clamped my hands around Harry's arm as if someone was going to pull me away from him. The nurse administered the injection and then we waited for the doctor to return. The medication began to work as Harry felt my grip loosen around his arm. The doctor returned along with a female. This is Dr. August. I felt it would be better if she examined you. We appreciate it Doctor, Harry said. I am going to take a sample of the fluids and then we will go from there. I let the doctor do everything she needed to do including give me another shot for the pain and a few stitches where Malik had torn me during his horrid assault. After the doctor finished and prepared to release me from the hospital, the police entered to finish asking me questions. I gave them all the information about what had taken place that evening. I had given them as much information about Malik as I could. I even told them everything she remembered him saying to me. Especially the threat of returning again. They were on their way to pick him up.

CHAPTER FIVE

They finally released me and I was depending upon Harry to get me home. Home I thought. I don't want to see that place, not tonight. What about your parents, I can take you to… He could hardly finish the sentence when I frantically begged him not to take me there. Harry offered to stay with me at my apartment, but I said no. So he offered his place to me instead. I accepted his offer. We left the hospital and road quietly to Harry's apartment. I was left wearing a hospital gown and no clothing of my own. Harry gave me a t-shirt and a pair of his pajama pants to where. I graciously accepted them. I changed into the garments and returned from the bathroom. I opened his bedroom door and eased out into the living room. I made you

some tea; I hope that's all right? Thank you, I
said as I eased down in the chair. The pain
became real to me when I couldn't sit
comfortably. Harry went into the bedroom to
retrieve a pillow from the bed. He returned and
helped me up, placed the pillow in the seat and
helped me down onto it. Is that better, he
asked? Yes, much, thank you. I sipped on my
tea as we both set to the table. Quietness
filled the room. It was an uncomfortable
silence. He didn't know what to say to me. I
didn't know what to say to him. So, I spoke
first to break the ice. Thank you so much for
showing up when you did. I wish I could have
been there sooner, he said. I felt the
awkwardness again and it showed on my face. Are
you sure you don't want me to call your family?
Yes, I'm sure. I won't be in your way too much

longer, I said to him. You are not in my way, he said as he reached for my hand across the table. I was slightly apprehensive about him touching me in that way. I endured his touch, but he noticed the change in my mood as he removed his hand away from mine. Are you ready to lye down now? I nodded my head. You can sleep in my room and I will take the sofa. No, I don't want to put you out of your bed. That's perfectly ok. You need to get some rest and I can take the sofa. I didn't argue with him at this point because I could feel sleep coming over me.

Harry made me comfortable in his bedroom and he headed into the living room to sleep on the sofa. He thought about why I would not allow him to call my family. I had my reasons. I did not want to involve them for obvious reasons,

"Kentrel". I was not ready to explain to my
parents why I was involved with a married man.
While Harry lay on the sofa, he wondered to
himself, what have I gotten my self involved in?
Why does this feel so right? I feel as if I
have known Maria all of my life. I feel like I
have to protect her. I hope she will be all
right. Just as he dosed off to sleep, he heard
her scream out. No! No! He jumped to his feet
and ran to the room. Maria! Maria! I was
reliving my attack from Malik. He turned on the
lights and I was able to see that it was not
Malik. Harry asked me if it was ok if he sat
with me. I agreed and allowed him to sit beside
the bed. Can I get you something, he said?
Yes, a drink? The stronger the better, I said.
That won't help you Maria. I just want to
forget Harry. You can't forget Maria, this has

happened to you and you have to deal with it.
Forgetting is not an option. Things like this
don't just go away, he said. I have always
believed in the phrase "what doesn't kill us
makes us strong" and I believe that this will
make you stronger. If anything it will make you
a little less trusting. You make it sound like
I asked for this to happen to me Harry. No
that's not what I am saying. I just said that
you were too trusting. You thought that you
knew Malik. You never thought that he would
have done this to you. Yeah, I never thought
that Kentrel would be such a dog, just like
Malik. Or maybe I just did not want to see him
for who he was. I think I want to sleep now
Harry. Thank you for everything. I will be
right outside if you need me. Good night Harry.
Good night Maria.

I woke up to the sound of Harry's voice coming from the other room. As I listened, I heard another male voice talking to Harry. I made an attempt to get out of bed but the pain was too much. When I looked up Harry was beside the bed ready to assist me. Is someone here I asked? Just one of my friends he said. I just saw him out. Lean on me and I'll help you. Do you need something for the pain, he asked? Yes I sure do. My arms were bruised from Maliks hands and my wrists were extremely sore. I needed Harry's help in more ways than one. When I emerged from the bathroom, Harry was there to help me back to his bed. I thanked him as I made myself as comfortable as I could under the circumstances. Maria would you like something to eat? Harry you have been so kind to me. I should let you get back to unpacking. You are

not in my way at all. You need someone right
now and I am more than happy to be that person.
However, you should allow me to call your folks.
No Harry. I can't deal with that right now. I
need to go home, would you take me please? Sure
if that's what you want. Yes, I think it would
be best. I have inconvenienced you enough.
Everybody needs some body Maria and you just
happened to need me right now. He went into the
kitchen to get me something for the pain and
juice. He returned to the bedroom and I was
sitting on the side of his bed. Here you are,
he said as he handed me a pain pill and the
glass of juice. Thank you Harry, you really are
a great guy. There are some of us left in the
world you know. I am so thankful for that, I
said with a slight smile. I handed him the
glass and realized that I did not have shoes or

slippers to where. I forgot that you carried me in last night. Don't worry, I will carry you again he said as he smiled.

Walking into the apartment was a very unsettling experience for me. I had hoped that I could handle the situation a little better than I did. When I walked through the door is was almost like reliving the night over. My legs gave way and Harry caught me. I've got you he said. I think that it's too soon for this, he said. No, I have to do this. Will you stay with me for a little bit? Sure, as long as you need me. I went into my room and feeling good to be in familiar surroundings, I took a nice soak in the tub. Harry called out to me a few times to see if I was all right. I'm here if you need me, he said. Ok I replied. Finally I emerged from the bedroom clothed in a large T-shirt and sweats. Harry had straightened my

living room from the tussle I had with Malik.

He didn't want to throw away my robe or under

garments due to fact that they might want them

for evidence. He asked for a bag to put them

in. I motioned to the cupboard door and Harry

took care of the clothes for me. I had not

given thought to the fact that it was a workday

and I had not called in to work. The phone

began to ring. Maria just stood there while it

rang. Do you want me to answer it? Yes, she

said. Hello. May I speak to Ms. Dolace,

please? May I tell her who's calling? This is

Mrs. George from her office. Hold on please.

It's your office, he said. I just stood there a

minute before taking the phone. Hello I said.

Maria, are you all right? Someone said that

they saw an ambulance and police at your place

last night and I have been calling all morning for you. What is going on? I was, I mean, I was, I dropped the phone as tears began to run down my face. Harry grabbed the phone and grabbed on to me at the same time. He could feel his heart was breaking for her at that moment. Hello ma'am, I'm a neighbor of Ms. Dolace. She was attacked yesterday evening and I have just brought her home from the hospital. Maybe now is not a good time to speak with her. I understand and what did you say your name was? Harry Stonewell ma'am. Well, tell Maria that I will inform the supervisor and we will check in on her later today. I will do that ma'am. Thank you for calling. He hung up the phone and walked Maria to the sofa. I'm calling your folks, what's the number. No, Harry. Yes, what is the number? 310-2020 I said. Harry dialed

the number and waited for someone to answer the
phone. Dolace residence. Hello Mr. Dolace my
name is Harry Stonewell and I am a neighbor of
your daughters. Hello Mr. Stonewell, and what
can I do for you? Mr. Dolace, I need you and
your wife to come to your daughters apartment,
she was attacked yesterday. Oh dear God, is she
all right? She was attacked. I think that you
all should come over. We will be right there.
Thank you for calling son. Thank you. He hung
up the phone and yelled for his wife. Audrey,
Audrey, he yelled. What is it Henry? Maria,
she's been hurt, we need to go to her. Oh God,
not my baby. Is she all right? I don't know
mother, but we need to go. Where is she? Is
she in the hospital? No she is at home. Mrs.
Dolace began praying for Maria as they drove.
All right, your parents are on their way, Harry

said. I know that you don't want to worry them
but you should not be alone. I'm not alone,
Harry, you're here. I know that, but you need
someone close to you. You need you parents
right now. I understand that you have to go
Harry, it's ok, and you can leave now. No, you
don't understand. I am not going anywhere. I
just feel that you need something more than me,
Maria. I can't take care of you like your
mother can. You have done a fine job so far,
Harry. Even if we have just met each other, I
feel as if I have known you forever. I feel the
same way. Thank you Harry. I don't know what I
would have done without you. Mr. and Mrs.
Dolace pulled up in front of Maria's apartment
and hurried themselves out of the car. Harry
met them at the door. Are you Harry? Yes sir,
thank you for calling us. Where is my baby,

Mrs. Dolace said as she went through the door? I'm right here Mama. Oh, my baby, what happened? I don't want to talk about it Mama. Harry nodded for Mr. Dolace to follow him outside. Once they were clear of the door, Mr. Dolace proceeded to ask questions. I wish you would talk to Maria first. You can see that she don't want to talk about it so I am counting on you to fill in the blanks for me son. You were good enough to call us, now be good enough to clue me in. Well, I saw Maria yesterday and realized that I knew her from church. You belong to Starlight? My mother does. Mrs. Whitney is my mother. Right, Sara and Audrey are good friends. You can't be Lil' Harry. Yes sir that's me. Ok Harry, what happen to my daughter and who the hell did it? Well, Maria and I spoke briefly and I told her that I would stop in on her. When I came over and was about to knock on the door it opened and a man came out and just brushed by me real quickly. That's when I heard crying from inside and I ran in and found her on the floor with her clothes torn off. Mr. Dolace was pacing quite angrily at this point. The bastard raped my daughter. Are you saying that he raped her? Yes sir, he did. I immediately called 911 to request an ambulance and the police. They took her to the hospital and. Why didn't someone call us last night? Sir, I have been trying to get her to call you all since last night. I had to force her to give me the number this morning. Thank you son, we are indebted to you for looking after our girl. Who is this creep? Did she know him? Yes sir, it appears the man is a friend of the guy she is dating. All right, I need a minute

to pull myself together before I go in, Mr.
Dolace said. Take all the time you need sir. I
will see you inside. Harry opened the door to
walk in. Maria lay in her mother's arms crying.
Shhhh, baby you're going to be fine. Just fine.
Harry walked over to the sofa and stooped down
in front of Maria. Do you want me to leave you
with your folks now? No, Harry please don't
leave. Stay here with me. She didn't want to
even be alone with her parents. He rubbed her
arm and smiled. Ok, I'll stay a while. Look, I
need to make a few calls. He walked over to the
phone to make his calls and to give them time to
talk.

CHAPTER SIX

On the other side of town, police closed in
on Malik. He answers the door with a smug
attitude. Are you Malik Watson, the police
office asked? Yeah that's me. Would you step
outside the door please? Maliks' wife Rainesse
came to the door. Malik, what's going on out
here? What's up officer is something wrong?
Please step outside the door. One of the
officers asked Rainesse to stay in the doorway.
Malik stepped outside the door and one of the
officers took his hand, handcuffed him and the
other read him his rights. What am I being
arrested for? I haven't done anything.
Rainesse stepped outside of the door. In an
angry tone she asked, Malik what did you do? He
looked up at her as if he was so innocent. You
are under arrest for aggravated rape and

assault. What? I didn't rape nobody. She
invited me in to her house, he said. She asked
for it. I didn't rape her man. The officer
continued to read him his rights while he
complained that he was being falsely accused.
Rainesse and nosy neighbors stood watching as
the police took her husband away.

Yet at Kentrel's house the phone was ringing
off the hook. Kentrel answered the phone. Man
your boy just got arrested, yelled Cedric,
another of Kentrel's friends. Arrested, who
are you talking about? Malik, man, the police
just arrested him. They said he raped some
chic. What? Rape? Who did he rape? Man they
said it's that chick you mess with. Maria?
Yeah man, that's her. Kentrel slammed the phone
down. Sheila looked at him with questions going
through her mind. Kentrel knew that Malik had

the hots for Maria and he told him that he would be flirting with death if he ever touched her. Kentrel paced the floor like a mad man. What is wrong honey? Malik was arrested a few minutes ago. I need to leave. Where are you going? I need to check on something. Enraged was not the word for Kentrel at this point. He was ready to kill. If this is true, Malik had better stay in jail. Man if he put his hands on her, I don't know what I might do to him. He pulled out his cell phone and dialed Maria's office. Childs/Anderson, may I help you? Maria Dolace, please. I'm sorry she isn't in today, would you like to leave a message? Kentrel hung up the phone. Oh damn, he said as he increased his speed.

As he pulled up to Maria's apartment, he noticed her parents car along with a black truck parked in the driveway. He jumped out of his vehicle and ran to the door. He just opened the door and rushed in. Maria! He called out as he rushed in. Mr. Dolace and Harry both stood up as to guard Maria from this intruder. I just heard that something happened to Maria, is she all right? Mrs. Dolace spoke to him. Kentrel, someone has hurt my baby. Kentrel walked around the two men and kneeled down in front of me and my mother. Just seeing her bruised cheek sent fire threw his body. He wanted to touch her but wasn't sure if it was all right. Get out, I whimpered. What? You heard me, get out. Maria, wait a minute, I'm here for you. Why do you want me to leave? I need to know what happened? I turned away from him. Maria, Cedric said that Malik was arrested for raping you. He took a deep breath. Is this true? Did

he touch you? She turned to look at him. Mrs.
Dolace placed her hand over her mouth. She knew
her daughter was attacked but she didn't know
she was raped. She didn't want to hear anymore
of what was being said. I sat up and looked at
him. Yes he did Kentrel. You told him to do it.
What, he said with disbelief? You know what I
am talking about Kentrel "you share everything".
That's what he told me. He said that you knew
he was here and…….. Before she could finish,
Harry stepped in. All right that's enough. You
need to leave. Who the hell are you? Someone
she wants here and you my friend are not. I'm
not your friend and don't you touch me. Maria
we need to talk. Mr. Dolace moved next to Harry
and in a demanding tone said, you had better go
now son. Kentrel looked at Maria with a sincere
look on his face, Baby why are you doing this to

me. I am here for you. Go home Kentrel, go
home to your wife. Wife, Mr. Dolace said with
anger in his voice! Yes, his wife, she
repeated. Now get out of my house Kentrel. The
love I once felt for him had now turned to
hatred. I could not stand the sight of him.
Now that it is out in the open, I could not even
face my parents. I could see the sadness in my
father's eyes as he looked down at me. But in
light of all I had been through, neither of my
parents said another word about Kentrel. I want
to know what happened, Mrs. Dolace demanded.
Harry had heard the statement that Maria gave to
the police at the hospital. But he felt it was
not his place to tell them, so he kept quiet. I
don't know if I can do this, I said as I held my
head. Just thinking of Malik and what he did to
me made me well aware of the pain I was

experiencing. The more I thought of him touching me the sicker I felt. Mama, I don't feel well I said as I tried to get up from the sofa. I want to lye down. Maria, there are no covers on your bed, Harry said. I used them to cover you last night. Harry would you mind helping me I said. I will help you honey, Mrs. Dolace said. No mama, I want Harry to do it. Come on I'll carry you? Maria's father sat to the table with his face in his hands. Mrs. Dolace walked over and sat across from him. This is not real, this just can't be real she said. My child is seeing a married man. And she was raped, Mr. Dolace announced. This is what happens when you turn your back on the Lord, Mrs. Dolace said. Mother please, Maria has not turned her back on God, Audrey. She's just---- Hell I don't know what she is doing. I should have known something was wrong when we stop seeing her as much, he said. The ringing of the phone interrupted the conversation. Mr. Dolace answered it. Hello he yelled. May I speak with Maria, please? Who is this? This is Gayle Mr. Dolace. Gayle and Maria became best friends while in high school. Franchesca Gayle Fairlane is 5 feet 3 ½ inches tall with light brown skin tone and straight black shoulder length hair. She has always worn her hair with a part down the middle and contouring the sides of her face. Gayle is engaged to her high school sweetheart Ronald J. Kirkshem, a private practice attorney. She never liked being called Franchesca so she convienced everyone to call her Gayle. She detects the anger in Mr. Dolace's voice as begins to speak to him. I'm just checking to see if she was ok. No she is not ok! She was raped. So, she is not ok. And he hung up the phone. Why did you do that Henry? She might not want anyone to know. Just like she didn't want anyone to know that she was having an affair with a married man, Audrey! I should have kicked his. HENRY! Mr. Dolace looked around at her and apologized. Audrey, I am sorry. I am so angry. I am angry that this happened, and I am angry that I don't even know who that child is in the other room. And did you know that she haven't even known Harry that long and she would prefer that he take care of her than us. What has happened to our child? I don't know Henry. I just don't know Mrs. Dolace said with sadness.

CHAPTER SEVEN

I waited as Harry found the bedding for me and straightened out my bed. Before I could climb into the bed I felt sick to my stomach. I turned and moved as fast as I could to the bathroom. Harry followed me. As I dropped to the floor and held my head over the toilet, Harry wet a wash cloth and pulled my hair back. He rubbed my back to try to ease the discomfort I was having. I felt even more humiliated to have him see me this way. This thought only brought additional tears as I hung over the rim of the toilet. Harry handed me the towel and I wiped my face and mouth. Are you ok now? I nodded yes as he helped me up from the floor. Mrs. Dolace was standing in the doorway of the bathroom watching. She hurt for her daughter and yet she could not make her feel better. She was at a lost for words. Can I do anything, she asked? No, I've got her, Harry said. Harry allowed me to lay my head on his chest, while he poured mouthwash into the cup on the sink. He put the cup to my mouth. Rinse with this sweetie, he said. I did as he asked while he held my hair back again. He allowed my hair to fall free as I stood up to face him. Tears began to run down my face again. I felt so helpless. He tried wiping them away with his hand. I wish I could take away all your pain Maria. I leaned into him and rested my head on his chest while holding on to him. He returned the embrace as Mrs. Dolace observed from the door. Harry gently kissed the top of my head. Come on and lye down for a little while. He released his hold and I looked up right into my mothers eyes. I headed straight to her arms.

My baby she said as she embraced me. They walked over to the bed and Mama helped me into the bed. I climbed in under the fresh sheets and drew myself up in a little ball. Can I get you anything, Harry asked? No just stay and keep me company. Do you want me to stay honey? No, just check on Daddy for me. Ok honey, Mrs. Dolace said. You get some rest ok? All right Mama. When Mrs. Dolace closed the door, I looked at Harry. That's why I didn't want you to call them. There were too many issues that they didn't know about. And now they know, because of me, he said. I'm sorry, I figured that they could do a better job of taking care of you than I could. Sometimes parents aren't the best people for the job Harry. I see what you mean. Harry pulled up a chair and sat beside my bed as he did the night before waiting for me to fall asleep. I drifted off to sleep as he watched me. His thoughts were soothing ones. What has your life been like, Maria, he thought to himself? He could only wonder about it. Mrs. Dolace knocked on the bedroom door, as Harry quietly walked over to open it. How is she? Asleep he said and walked outside to talk to her. She feels she has let you all down, he said. Well, an affair with a married man is a big let down don't you think, Mr. Dolace said? In consideration of the state she is in right now, the affair should be put on the back burner and you all need to help her cope with what has happened to her. Let's take a seat and talk about this. I need to tell you all what this creep has done to her. As they took a seat at the table, Harry said I hope you all can handle this, cause Maria is going to

need you now more than ever. They both had
frightening looks on their faces. I'm only
telling you this because I was with her in the
hospital and I was the one who found her right
after it happened. This creep tore your
daughter apart and I mean physically. The
emergency room doctor had to give her stitches.
They also took blood to see if he has infected
her in any way. The veins in Mr. Dolaces' face
were huge. Mrs. Dolace covered her face to hide
her tears. Mr. Dolace walked over to her to
console her. Look, he also threatened to come
back again. So, lets hope that the police have
arrested him by now. So when I said that the
affair should be the least of your concern, I
truly meant it. When the reality of what has
happened to her hits home she might really fall
apart. Having to even face the both of you,

have taken a lot out of her. She never wanted you to know. Think about how she will feel facing the people outside this apartment. If the two of you are this critical of her, she won't stand a chance on the outside. You have to pull together for her sake. Put your fears and emotions and all the baggage you want to throw at her somewhere else, because this is going to take some time. What are you, some kind of Psychiatrist or something, Mr. Dolace asked? Yes I am a Psychologist. I understand what Maria is going through and what she will probably go through for a long time. That's why I am telling you all of this. They both sighed. Mrs. Dolace sent her husband to pick up their youngest daughter from the bus and she would stay with Maria. Harry left to take a shower and change clothes. He promised Maria he would be there when she woke up and he knew how important it was for promises to be kept right now. So he told Mrs. Dolace that he would come back. He left his phone number so that she would be able to reach him.

CHAPTER EIGHT

Gayle sat at her desk with tears streaming down her face. She wanted to be with her friend and help her through this. She was upset that her friend had been hurt. She tried to pull herself together before moving from her seat. She walked into the supervisor's office and she could hardly get a word out because of the tears. Milton passed her a few tissues and asked her to calm down so that he could understand what is going on with her. The others in the office saw Gayle crying and were tuned in for the gossip. It's Maria. What about Maria? I know that she was attacked or something like that. Yes sir, she was attacked and raped yesterday. I just talked with he father. Outside the door, you could hear the rest of the office buzzing with what was overheard. Milton got up and closed the door. Calm down Gayle. Are you sure? Yes sir. He sat down to his desk and pulled out his Rolodex. He dialed Maria's number. Hello, Mrs. Dolace answered. This is Milton Dawson, and I am Maria's boss, with whom am I speaking? This is Mrs. Dolace, Maria's mother. Mrs. Dolace, I just received some rather disturbing news and I am following up on it. Is it true that Maria was attacked and raped? Yes Mr. Dawson, it is true. Under the circumstances, Mrs. Dolace, how is she? Not very good right now, but that is to be expected, I really can't tell you very much right now. She is not doing much talking. Well, I am very sorry that this happened to her and please tell her to take as much time as she needs. We are all praying for her and if there is anything we can do just let us know. Thank you for calling Mr. Dawson and I will be sure to tell her. Milton turned to Gayle. Well, I'm sorry to say Gayle, you were right. Gayle started to cry again. Why don't you take the rest of the day off Gayle? Thank you Milton she said as she sobbed into the tissues. While walking to her desk several of the others tried to question her about what they had heard. She told them that she would call them once she saw Maria and headed out of the office.

Kentrel was livid. He wanted Malik and he wanted him bad. The only thing that kept him from getting his hands on him was the fact that he was still in jail. After riding and talking with a few of his other friends, he went home. Sheila was there waiting for him and wanting to know what was happening with Malik. Did he rape somebody, she said? Yes he did, Sheila. What is wrong with him? Has he lost his mind? I don't want to talk about this anymore, Kentrel said. What is your problem? I just asked you about Malik. I said I don't want to talk about it. Why not Kenny? He didn't answer. Well I heard that it was you little tramp. Fire burned through Kentrel when she spoke those words. He tried with everything in him to ignore her. He even got up to walk out of the room. She followed him. What's wrong Kenny, you angry cause she gave it up to Malik? That was the last straw. He turned and slapped her across the face. He grabbed her by the shoulders and looked directly into her eyes. You should learn to leave shit alone when people ask you to woman. Then he let her go and walked out of the house. Sheila was so shocked that he had hit her. He had never laid a hand on her throughout their entire marriage. Even when they split up it was her that did all of the kicking and hitting. This girl must really mean something to him, she thought to herself. As she continued to rub her face and pull herself together, she said out loud. I have some serious thinking to do about this marriage.

Meanwhile, Harry returned to Maria's apartment. Mrs. Dolace was standing in the window just looking out as Harry walked up to the door. She went to the door and let him in. How is she doing? She is still sleeping. Good he said. She didn't get much sleep last night. Um, Mrs. Dolace said. In the back of her mind she was wondering what was the connection between Harry and her daughter. He could tell by the look on her face that she was wondering about him. I spoke with my mom and she said to tell you that she is praying for all of you. Your mom, Mrs. Dolace said with question. Yes ma'am, Sara Whi… You can't be Lil' Harry? Yes ma'am that's me, he said with laughter. Good Lord boy you have turned out to be quite a nice looking man. Thank you ma'am. Now what are you doing with my daughter? Well, really we just met, before this happened. I don't know how to help her with this Harry. Patience and prayer ma'am that will do it every time. You seem to know a lot about these things. Well, living in the big city you see and hear about everything that's going on. At the clinic where I worked, we had to deal with all types of cases. I must tell you that rape cases ranked the highest. Well, I promised Maria, I would be there when she woke up so, let me peak in on her. Sure Harry, you do that. While Harry walked away to

see about Maria, the doorbell rang. Mrs. Dolace
went to open the door. Hello Gayle. Hello Mrs.
Dolace she said as she reached out to give her a
hug. How are you? Oh, I have been better,
honey. May I come in? Yes, come on in. Is
Maria here? Yes dear she is asleep. I had to
come once I heard what happened. I was so upset
when I heard. Yes we all are. All we can do is
be here for her. The door of Maria's bedroom
opened and Harry eased out and closed the door
behind him. Gayle, this is Harry. Harry this
is Maria's best friend, Gayle. They also work
together. It's good to meet you Gayle. It's
nice to meet you Harry. Is she still sleeping,
Mrs. Dolace said? Yes ma'am. Right as the
words left his lips, Maria screamed out. No!
No Malik, No! Harry turned and ran back into
the room. I was fighting in my sleep. He

called to me as he tried to stop me from fighting. Mrs. Dolace and Gayle ran to the other side of the bed. They were all calling my name. But I only responded to Harry's voice. Once I opened my eyes and they made contact with his, I reached for him. Harry I cried, is he gone, make him go away Harry, make him go away. I've got you Maria. Shhhhh, he's not here. Look, he's not here. There is your mother and Gayle is here. See everyone here loves you and no one will hurt you. But I held on to him tightly as he sat down in the bed beside me. I buried my face into his strong chest and gripped his shirt. Mrs. Dolace stood back with one hand on her mouth and the other on her chest. Gayle put her arm around Mrs. Dolaces' shoulder as tears fell from he own face. Harry rubbed his hand across my back in an attempt to calm me down. He made himself comfortable on the bed while he held on to me. I cried for a little while, as I lay in his arms feeling so helpless. You know the only way to get through this is to face your demons. Sobbing, I asked, " What do you mean"? You have to face the thing that hurt you. You mean I have to face Malik? I want him dead! I just want him dead. I want him dead. Shhhh, that is not healthy thinking. What Malik did to me is not healthy. Just rest Maria. Don't think just rest. You need to get your strength. Harry knew that she needed to be strong for the fight she would undertake when she fought this bastard in court. Being in Harry's arms became more comfortable for the both of them. He was her hero right now. He felt responsible for her and she letting him into her world. You lay right here and I will

get you something to eat. I'm not hungry. Yes
you are, you just don't know it. Harry walked
out of the room to discuss getting Maria
something to eat. Gayle volunteered to go and
pick up something. Mrs. Dolace went into the
kitchen to prepare something hot to drink.
Harry returned to Maria and she was sitting up
in the bed waiting. Neither of them realized
that a bond was forming between them. She
trusted his presence. Everything is taken care
of. Your mother is making tea and Gayle is
getting you something to eat. I did not answer.
You have to eat something all right. You can't
go with out food. This will help your body to
heal he said. Some things can't be healed I
said, with anger in my voice. Only if you allow
them Harry responded. I gave a little smile.
Is that a smile? Wait, I think it was, come on

give it to me, come on. I had to laugh as he

coaxed another smile from my lips. That's

beautiful, he said. I blushed. For the first

time since the rape I saw him as a man. Maybe

it was the way he looked at me. I felt awkward

and he noticed it. I'm sorry, he said. I

didn't mean to make you feel uncomfortable.

Then there was a funny ringing sound. Harry

pulled the cell phone from his pants pocket and

looked at the screen. He turned it off and put

it back into his pocket. You need to get out of

this bed and put on some clothes, Harry said to

her in an attempt to lighten the atmosphere. I

really don't feel like moving right now. Well

you have to, cause you my friend, according to

this paper he pulled from his other pants

pocket, have a doctors appointment today. No I

don't, I exclaimed. I didn't make any

appointments. No you didn't, he said. I made it for you. This is something you need to do and it has to be done today. Why and who is this appointment with? Well, it's with a counselor at the hospital. I don't need counseling. I just want to be left alone. I want everyone to just go away and leave me alone. Why Maria? So that you can hide out and close everyone out? That's not going to happen. At least not today. You can run away if you want to but we aren't going anywhere. I sulked and pouted for a little while. I realized that Harry was not leaving the room and I eased myself from the bed and walked slowly to the bathroom. That's my girl, I heard Harry say as I made it to the bathroom door. I stopped in my tracks but did not turn around. Just call me if you need me, Harry said, I'll be right here. I went into the bathroom and closed the door. I

ran the bath water and eased myself into the

tub. I had not noticed how dark the bruises had

gotten on her arms. Oh my God I yelled. Harry

jumped to his feet and ran to the door. Maria!

He said as his hand touched the doorknob.

What's wrong? My arms, Harry, my arms. Harry

opened the door. What? What's wrong with your

arms? Look at them, just look at them I cried.

It's ok. Just don't look at them. You know, he

said as he kneeled down to the tub wiping my

tears away, this will go away just like the

memory of all of this will. You have got to

fight to get your life back. You can do this.

You can, you know that don't you? I was closing

off my world again. I my pulled my knees up to

my chest and grabbed them with my arms and

cried. Let it out baby; just let it out. Not

realizing that I was allowed Harry to see me
naked, I allowed him to touch my back with his
hand. Harry reached for the towel and soap. He
lathered the towel and proceeded to sponge soap
across my back and shoulders. It's going to be
all right, he said. Just relax. I leaned my
head onto his arm and allowed him to help me
with my bath. Maria had a beautiful body. She
was fine and Harry had already made that
assumption the first day he saw her at church.
He made the connection again at that moment but
for her sake he had to remove his feelings. He
took one arm and gently ran the sponge over it
and then the other. He took his hand and gently
lifted my chin to bath my neck. When he came to
my breast he had to stop breathing for a moment.
You can handle this he said to himself. *Just be
yourself*. He ran the sponge over the top of one

breast and then the other. He cupped one and bathed under it and then the other. Harry did not want to hurt me in any way so instead of lifting my legs he just ran the sponge over my legs while submerged in the water. He bathed my feet and turned to me to give me the sponge. Maria lay there looking so beautiful and peaceful. Under any other circumstance this would be a sight to turn any man on. But he could not go there. He heard a knock at the bedroom door and the sound of it opening. Mrs. Dolace entered the room and noticed it was empty. Maria, Harry, is everything all right. Yes, we'll be out shortly, Harry said. Mrs. Dolace didn't know what to make of the situation, but nevertheless she closed the door and left them to what they were doing. All right madam, I will leave you to finish up, Harry said as he placed his hand on the tub to help himself up. I reached out to stop him from getting up. What is it, he said? Why, I asked with a look of uncertainty on my face. Why what? Why are you here? Why are you helping me like this? I don't know Harry said. I really don't know. I leaned up and kissed him on the cheek and lingered for a moment. Then I placed a soapy hand on his face and kissed him on the lips. Harry returned my kiss but only for a moment. You need to finish your bath he said as he stood and walked out of the room. Harry closed the door and stood there for a moment. *What just happened*, he said to himself? *Did she just kiss me or was I just.* The opening of the bathroom door broke his thoughts. All done, I said as I entered the room draped in a towel. Ok. Harry said, I'll get out of here so that you can get dressed. Harry? Yes? It's all right. What's all right? You're being here with me. I know Maria. I really mean it, I said. Harry was taken by surprise by her forwardness. *Is this the same person who just cried because of the bruises on her arms? Maybe she is stronger than I think.* Harry? Yes, he said as he was brought back to the reality of the moment. Are you here because you pitty me? No he exclaimed. Then why are you here with me? I told you, I can't explain it. I don't know. You have this effect on me and I can't seem to figure out what it is. It's like I know you and you seem to know me. Yeah, I get that feeling too. It's very comfortable. Well you need to get dressed, and I will check on the food. I watched him leave the room. *Did I just kiss him? Why did I do that? I must be out of my mind, she thought to herself. I don't even know myself anymore.* I began to get dressed. I was finding it harder and harder to face people, other than Harry. Maybe because this was the lowest point I had ever had, and he was there with me. If he has seen the worst of me what else is there, I thought out loud? I finally emerged from the bedroom and everyone turned to look at me. This really made me feel uneasy. I tugged at my shirt and moved slowly towards the table. Harry moved in to assist me. His actions had not gone unnoticed by all. Mr. Dolace had returned but Angel was not with him. Where is Angel, I asked? I dropped her off at Aunt Maura's house. You didn't tell them did you? Well yeah, Mr. Dolace said. Daddy why? I don't want anyone to know. I don't want them to know I said again as I planted my face into Harry's chest. Shhhhh, he said, just breathe Maria. Take a deep breath and breathe. I did as he asked. See isn't that better? I nodded my head up and down. Harry escorted me over to the table and sat me down in a chair with a pillow for my comfort. Mrs. Dolace he said, would you get some utensils please? Sure Harry. Gayle knew that Chinese was my favorite food so she purchased just about everything I liked. I just looked at the food in front of me and was not even the least bit hungry. I took several small bites and then just sat there. Harry sat to the table with me. You are not eating I said. I know, he said. I will eat when you finish. I don't want to eat alone. So Harry got a plate and put food on it. Can I get anyone else a plate he said? No you go on and eat Mr. Dolace said; we will take care of ourselves. Harry took several bites of food

and when he looked up I was smiling at him.
Wow, he said what did I do to deserve that?
Tell me so that I can do it again. Nothing I
said as I tilted my head to the side and brushed
my hair away from my bruised face. Mr. Dolace
noticed the exchange of quiet smiles between the
two of them. He could not tell if he felt good
about the exchange or not. But nevertheless she
was smiling and that alone was good. While they
ate, Harry's phone rang out again. This time he
answered it. This is Harry, he said. The voice
on the other end was definitely a female because
I could hear her talking quite loudly. Harry
did not say a word. Finally he just hung up the
phone. I eyed him with a questioning look, but
didn't question him. *If he wants to talk about
it he will*, I thought to myself. Ok we need to
go he said. Maria has an appointment. Mr. and

Mrs. Dolace turned to look at each other. What appointment? I'm going to see a counselor at the hospital, I said. Do you want us to go with you, Mrs. Dolace asked? No, Harry is taking me. Is there something you two aren't telling us Mr. Dolace asked? No. They both said at the same time as they looked at each other. Will you all be here when we get back, I asked? Do you want us to, asked Mrs. Dolace? Gayle butted in and said that she would wait for her and stay if she wanted her to. Good, I'd like that. Wait here and I'll get the truck, Harry said as he walked out of the door. While he was on his way to get the truck his phone rang again. Man she is just getting on my nerve, he said out loud. Hello, he said with an attitude. Where are you Harry? Why haven't you returned my calls? I have been busy Gina. What do you want? I just want to talk to you. We said everything before I left Washington. There is nothing else to say. I was wrong, Gina said, and I want to apologize for everything. Did you hear me Harry? I heard you Gina. I hear you every time you say you're sorry. Frankly I have heard it enough. Stop calling me Gina. Goodbye. Harry hung up the phone and turned it off. I have had enough of this.

CHAPTER NINE

He jumped into his truck and just as he was backing out, Travis and Eddie pulled up behind him. They exchanged pleasantries and he told them he had something to do. We will check you out later, Eddie said. Eddie is a colleague from the hospital and Travis is a friend of Eddies. Eddie is six feet tall and fine as a man can be. He is as handsome as Harry is. Travis is not far behind the fine handsome brother portrait. His smooth creamy complexion skin and medium brown wavy hair fit well with his 5 foot 7 inch masculine stature. Harry was rushing them off so that he could make Maria's appointment. Sure man, give me a call, Harry said. They pulled out of the driveway and took off. Harry backed out behind them and pulled up in front of Maria's door and honked the horn.

Feeling very uncomfortable leaving my house for the first time since last night's attack, I felt like everyone would be looking at me. Knowing how painful it would be to walk fast, I put up a front and moved to the truck as if there was no pain at all. Harry met me at the door of the truck. Be yourself sweetie, you don't have anything to hide. Just be your self. *It seems as if he could read my mind*, I thought. I knew little about Harry's educational background, so him being able to read my body language was strange to me. She just knew that he had said that he was working up state somewhere. He made me comfortable and strapped me in and he headed around to the drivers' side and jumped in. They rode in silence for a little while. Then he turned on the radio. A Latin artist was playing. I like him I said. You into Latin music? A little, I said. I will have to play

for you sometime. You play in a band or

something. Well, we have a little group that my

friends and I put together. I would love to

hear you play. Well I mostly sing. Really, well

you will have to sing for me some time. I would

be happy to. They pulled up to the hospital

parking lot and he asked if I wanted to get out

in front. No, I'd like to walk with you if you

don't mind. I like the way you are handling

this Maria. It shows promise that you will get

past this. When Malik is dead, I will be past

this. It is not healthy for you to speak like

that. Whatever I mumbled. Harry noticed the

attitude she displayed. They took their time

and walked to the building. Harry walked up to

the desk and the nurse spoke to him by name.

Good morning Dr. Stonewell. Good morning Amy,

would you inform Helen that I am here with Ms.
Dolace? Sure Doctor. You didn't tell me you
were a doctor. No I didn't. She is ready for
you doctor. Thank you Amy. She began to see
him in a different light. Her mood became quiet
and observant. She had learned one thing over
the last few days, which applied to two men.
You can never tell anything about a man. Malik
she thought a friend harmed her in the worst way
and Harry a stranger protects her and cares for
her in the most loving way. Go figure. They
walked down a long corridor and finally through
a door. A woman met them on the other side.
Hello Harry she said. Hello Helen. This is my
friend Maria. Hello Maria. Hello I said very
shyly. Maria, Helen is the counselor I told you
about today. She is going to help you to get
through this crisis. I was quiet. I will let

you ladies talk and I will return in an hour.
If you need me before then just beep me. I'm
sure every thing will be fine, just fine, Helen
said. Come on in Maria. Have a seat. Helen
told me a few things about herself. Then she
just wanted me to talk to her. I of course had
nothing to say. This is about you honey, and
what ever is said here stays here. I know about
the rape and I know everything that Harry has
told me. But I want to hear from you. I want
you to tell me what you are thinking and feeling
right now. I am angry. Good Helen said. Why
is that good? It is good that you are angry.
At least it is something. Sometimes women who
have been raped feel like they did something
wrong and they are told that they asked for the
rape to happen. Nothing is further from the
truth. No one asked to be raped. No one wants

to be violated. That's how I feel. See, if I had not of let Malik in he would not have raped me. You are blaming yourself Maria and that is something we are going to change. The person to blame is Malik. You are going to shift the blame where it belongs. You trusted a friend and he broke that trust. You did nothing wrong. Society has made us feel that when something happens to us it is our fault. This is not true. They talked for some time and finally the hour was over. I felt a little better that I could get some of the feelings I had out in the open. Especially the ones I had about killing Malik. I thanked Helen and waited for Harry to come and get me. When he walked up I was smiling. Wow, there is that smile again. This must have been a wonderful session for you. It was good. I like talking to her. She understands what I am feeling. When is your next appointment? Monday. Great. We have one more stop to make before we leave. I want you to see Dr. Azule. Who is he? He is an OB. Why do I need to see him? Well you did not get the shot the night of the rape. What shot? Just in case Malik made you pregnant. I thought I would be sick at that exact moment. Sorry, I was in my doctor's mode. I didn't mean to be so blunt. They walked to the elevator and stepped on. Harry pressed the button to go to the fourth floor. They stepped off and walked to the desk. Hello Doctor Stonewell, hello Cheryl. Doctor Azule is waiting for you, she said. Thank you Cheryl. They walked through another door and straight into the Doctors office. Have a seat, Harry said. I will be right back. Harry returned with the doctor and a nurse. The doctor was holding Maria's file from last night's hospital visit. How are you feeling Maria? I am feeling fine. How about the pain? Are you in any pain? Yes, I said. Where is the pain? Well, it is in the lower part of my body, she said shyly. I am sure it's the stitches that are giving you all the trouble. They will soon dissolve. You were given a shot of antibiotic last night and I will give you another one today. The nurse left and returned with two syringes on a tray. Would you lower your pants for a moment please, she asked? I did as she as asked. The injections were administered. We will check you out when you come to see Helen on Monday. When you finish your session with Helen, just come right up here to see me all right. All right. I said.

CHAPTER TEN

As we walked to the vehicle, I was very quiet. So, you're a doctor. Yes. What kind of doctor? Psychiatric, he said cautiously. I see. I became quiet and thought she knew what the attraction was for him. *I am just another case for him, she thought to herself.* So, am I considered your patient? No, I never treat my friends. Do you think I need psychiatric help? No I think you need counseling. I think of counseling as a coping tool. Helen is a therapist not a psychiatrist. There is a difference. I see. I am with you because I want to be. We all have choices Maria and I choose to be here with you. I consider you my friend and I hope that I am yours. Yes you are Harry and a real good one at that. Let's go

home then, he said with a smile. All right,
let's go home.

Back at the house, Maria's parents were
nervous, waiting for their daughter to return.
They heard the truck pull up and met them at the
door. Her parents saw that Maria's face was a
little lighter with expression. What ever
happened was a good thing and her parents were
pleased. Why don't you come home with us for a
while, Mr. Dolace said? No daddy, I want to
stay here. You can check up on me in the
morning. Gayle and Harry will be here, won't
you guys? Yes, they both said. You all have
been great and I really appreciate it. I have
over come my fear of staying in my own home and
to get my life back. If I leave, I will be
running away from what happened and I don't want
to run, Daddy. I am willing to fight my demons

and she looked at Harry. What ever Harry has brought to her life was surly positive. Gayle was in awe of this new thing. She needed answers about Harry. But was unsure of how to ask. Harry has become my very good friend and I know that he and Gayle will take good care of me and help me through the night. You need to get my little sister and give her a big hug and kiss for me ok? I love you both. They gave her a hug and kiss and said good night.

I turned to Gayle and Harry, well what do we do? They looked at each other. Well I'm hungry I said. Is there any food left? *This was promising* Harry thought. *She has an appetite that is great*. I tell you what, Gayle said. I will run back to my place and pick up a few things and I will be back. You all want me to pick up something? As she was looking for her purse, she caught the two of them looking at each other. She definitely had questions for Maria. No, nothing I said. Nothing for me either, Harry said. All right, I will be back soon. Gayle walked out the door and Maria and Harry were still smiling at each other. I need a drink and a shower he mumbled. He went over to the refrigerator and retrieved a bottle of juice. Can I get you something? A little company over here I said. Maria had walked over to the sofa and took a seat. I had the remote for the television in my hand. We could watch a movie I said. There was a knock at the door. Maria jumped. Take it easy, Harry said. He got up and went to the door. It's just my friend Eddie. He opened the door. Man we have been waiting on you for hours. Oh no, I forgot, Harry said. Look, I apologize, I have been tied

up and I just can't hang right now. Harry? I
called out. If you need to leave, I'll be fine.
Hello, pretty lady. Maria this is Eddie. Eddie
this is Maria. Hi Eddie, come on in Maria said.
Harry stepped aside and allowed Eddie to come
in. Nice place you have here. Thank you.
Forgive me if I don't get up, I said. No
problem. I saw Harry's truck and. You were
nosy and wanted to see why it was parked here
right, Harry said. Well, you know me, Eddie
said with a little laugh. I'm sorry man; I need
to be here right now. I will have to take a
rain check on that game. Harry, you can go with
your friends. I will be fine. Gayle will be
back shortly. Go! Are you sure? Yes. Look,
take this number and if for any reason, I don't
care what it is, you dial it. You promise? I
promise. He bent down on his knees to her at

the sofa and quietly said, "Hug"? I was eager
to fall into his arms. Ok   I'll go but I don't
think it is a good idea. Harry made sure the
door was locked as he left with Eddie.

Neither of them knew that Kentrel was down
the street watching. No sooner than Harry's
truck got out of sight did Kentrel pull up to
Maria's door. Being that he had his own key, he
didn't need to knock. I heard the door and was
about to loose my mind, until I saw Kentrel's
face. I let out a deep breath as he walked into
the apartment.   What are you doing here? Baby
I needed to see if you were all right. I will
never be all right again because of you and
Malik. Don't say his name Maria cause when I
get my hands on him he is a dead man. Maria
looked at him with great surprise. You are
telling me that you didn't have anything to do

with him being here? I had no idea he was here.

I swear it. I have always told him that if he

ever touched you I would kill him. I don't know

what to believe any more. I do know that we

can't go on anymore Kentrel. I can't be with

you any more. Kentrel thought his old tactics

would work on me, but I could not stand his

touch. When he saw the bruises on my arms, he

went cold. Malik did this to you? This is

nothing compared to the rest of my body. Malik

is a monster and he doesn't deserve to live, I

said. But it is not my decision to end his life

or keep him alive. I am responsible for me now.

I have to live for me. Do you understand that,

Kentrel? I do, but I don't want to. I stood up

right in front of Kentrel. Your friend tried to

take my life from me right there on my floor.

He dragged you along with him. He made me feel

as though I was a game for the two of you.
Kentrel stood there staring at the floor. He
ripped my clothes off my body and raped me
Kentrel. He also threatened to come back for
more. How do I get over that? Tell me? How do
I look at your face without seeing or thinking
about him? Answer me, I yelling. You're
telling me what you want but what about what I
want? I want for this to have never happened.
Can you give that back to me? He looked into
her eyes and then on the floor. I didn't think
so. I want you to go Kentrel. Give me my key
and leave. Kentrel took the door key off of his
ring and placed it on the table. I'm sorry
Maria. I am so sorry that he did this to you.
His face was sad and I thought I saw a tear fall
down his cheek. But I could not feel his
sorrow. I had my own to deal with. Kentrel

walked out of my door and got into his vehicle.

He just sat there with his face in his hands. I

closed the door and locked it. Harry didn't

feel good about leaving her. He had decided

that he would ditch the guys and turn back.

Kentrel was backing out as he was pulling up.

He jumped out of the truck and ran to the door.

Maria? Maria? Open the door it's me, Harry. I

opened the door, and he grabbed me. Are you ok?

I saw his car and I thought. ……. Kentrel is no

threat; it's his friend that is the threat.

Kentrel saw them embrace and his hurt doubled in

size. So, he said, she has someone else. Harry

looked back to see Kentrel move slowly down the

road. Did you let him in? He had his key, I

said. You need to change the locks, Harry said

in an angry tone. I have the key now. You

still need to change the locks. I decided not

to challenge the issue. I knew something was wrong, Harry said. I couldn't shake the feeling and that's why I came back. Girl what are you doing to me, he said? You have connected with my soul and I feel things that I have never… He stopped talking as he realized that he had said too much. I was standing looking at him and amazed. Harry openly said oh hell, come here. He put his arms around me and just held me. Harry, I said as I returned the embrace? Yes, he replied? What are we doing? I don't know, he said as he leaned me away from his chest. He stammered over his words. Harry? Harry took a deep breath and answered, yes Maria? Shut up and kiss me. Harry grinned and said, gladly. He leaned into me and placed his lips to mine. His hands left my waist and he placed them gently on my face. He was thinking of the kiss

at the bathtub. We need to stop, he said. This
is not good for you. Yes it is, I said. I am
supposed to be getting back to being myself
right? Well, yes you are, but. But nothing,
what better way than dive right back into it. I
still feel Harry. I don't know if I can forget
what happened to me, but I still have feelings.
Maria, stop it. This is serious. I turned and
walked into my bedroom and closed the door.
Jesus, I knew this was a bad idea, Harry said.
He went to the door and knocked on it. Maria?
Maria? Can I come in? I did not answer. Harry
turned the knob and opened the door. I lay in
her bed curled with one of my pillows pulled
tightly to my chest. Harry walked over to me.
He sat on the bed and pulled the hair away from
my face to look at me. I know you think that
this is what you need, but it isn't, I promise

you it isn't. I don't know what you think you are going to prove by throwing yourself at me or any other man. It won't change what happened to you. I was unmoved by his words. Maria, talk to me. I don't want to hurt you any more than you have been hurt. Do you understand what I'm saying to you? I knew she should say something to him, but I just couldn't. I felt dirty and ashamed. Harry felt that he had set progress back. He had a very concerned look on his face. He thought about all of the things he would tell the family members of rape victims at the clinic. He was doing the complete opposite. *If I were her husband, what would I tell him to do?* Do you want to be alone, he said? I still didn't answer. Harry walked out of the room and pulled the door in a little. I lay there as I began to replay the scene from the previous evening. I could almost feel Malik's hands on my body. I closed my eyes in an attempt to shut out the scene she had just replayed. I could hear myself scream for him to stop. I felt so dirty. How could I think that Harry would want me after knowing what that dog did to me? How could anyone want me? I jumped from the bed and flew into the bathroom and closed the door. I didn't take time to undress myself. I got into the tub and turned it on. Water hit my face and began to go everywhere. I felt as if I were drowning. Harry heard the water and went to investigate. He found her in shower gasping for breath. He turned off the water and pulled a towel from the cabinet and tried to drape it around her. I screamed out NO! NO! Leave me alone, as I slid down into the tub with my arms closed around my body as if I was trying to protect myself. I was crying like I had done the night of the rape. Let me help you Maria. Please let me help you. The fight seemed to have gone out of her now. I let him drape the towel around me and lift me from the tub. He dried my face and hair and began pulling off the wet clothes. I trembled as the cold air met my wet body. He grabbed another dry towel and began drying off the upper portion of my body. Harry was tired and yet he kept going. He reached for my pants to pull them off and I jumped back. Ok, ok, he said, why don't you handle that and I will look for something dry for you to put on. Harry left me in the bathroom. He went to her dresser drawer and pulled a T-shirt from one drawer and under garments from another. He pulled open several other drawers looking for pants. When he pulled open the last drawer, there he found several beautiful negligées. He quickly closed the drawer and went the closet door. There he found warm ups and pulled a pair from the wall. He walked into the bathroom and I hurriedly pulled the towel up to my body. The comfortable zone they had previously had disappeared. It was as if he was a stranger and she didn't know him. I decided to push him away. Harry saw how she shut her parents out and he knew that if she wanted to do the same to him, that it would not be hard for her. He decided to hand her the clothes and leave her to get dressed. I was taking exceptionally long to come out of the bathroom. Harry knocked on the door. I wiped the tears from my face and opened the door. All better now, he said. I tried to smile but it wasn't working for her. I did not feel desirable. Gayle returned and was ringing the doorbell. Harry went to let her in. I'm back she said. How are things? Harry groaned and said not good. Not good at all. What happened? Everything was going fine when I left. Things have changed, Harry said. What happened? We just had a few unpleasant scenes. It's rather personal. If you don't mind me asking Harry, just what is the nature of your relationship? Right now I can't even tell you that Gayle. She has never mentioned you to me, Gayle said. I know, he said. How long have you been seeing each other? Before he could attempt to answer her, his phone rang. He pulled it from his pocket. Hello, he said. Gina not now all right. I will call you when I am available to talk to you. But now is not a good time. Gayle left him to his phone call and walked into my room.   I was sitting in a chair, looking out of the window.   Maria, Gayle called to me, but I didn't answer.   She walked around the chair.   I sat looking out the window with a stream of tears falling from my eyes.   Oh Maria, Gayle said as she kneeled down to me.   What can I do? Give me my life back, I said.   I wish I could honey, I wish I could.   Harry was standing at the door but did not enter.   He just listened. You will get through this Gayle said.   How? Who's gonna want me now?   Who Gayle?   Harry could not believe the words that came from his mouth.   He was thinking the words but didn't realize that they had actually come from his mouth.   I want you, he said.   I quickly turned to look at him and Gayle stood up.   Did you hear me?   I said I want you Maria.   I have since the first day I saw you.   Nothing has happened to change that; he continued to say as he walked over to her. Gayle walked over to the door to give them some privacy. Harry kneeled down in front of me. He took my hands and told me again, I want you in my life. If you will have me. I cried. Oh Harry, I said. Harry lifted my chin. Do you want me in your life Maria? Gayle's eyes welled up with water as she witnessed the display of emotions between Harry and Maria. Yes, Harry I do. I want you in my life. Harry leaned into me and kissed me gently on the lips. Gayle covered her mouth as tears ran down her face. She was happy for Maria. She never felt good about Maria's relationship with Kentrel, but it was not her decision to make for her friend. She eased out of the room and closed the door. Let's just take it slow, he said. I just want you to know that I don't plan on going anywhere. You are going to heal

mentally and physically. We will get to know

each other on many levels and we have an

eternity to do it. Maria did not understand

that she had just been asked to be his for the

rest of her life. One day at a time he said.

If you promise not to go anywhere neither will

I. Oh, I promise doctor, I promise. I fell

into the arms that I had become accustom to over

the past few hours. In the living room, Gayle

was wondering if she should leave them alone.

Harry and Maria emerged from the bedroom with

smiles of contentment on their faces. I can see

that everything is well. Yes they both said. I

walked over to Gayle and gave her the biggest

hug. Thank you for being here with me Gayle.

I'm always here for you. I'm hungry I said,

lets order pizza. Great Gayle said as she wiped

the tears away from her eyes.

CHAPTER ELEVEN

Mr. and Mrs. Dolaces' ride home was a quiet one. Each of them had their own thoughts of Maria and what she had done to her life. Mr. Dolace was still angry and wanted to get his hands on both Kentrel and Malik. Mrs. Dolace was hurt and saddened by the fact that Maria lied to them about Kentrel. She sighed as a tear ran down her face. Henry put his arm around her and pulled her closer to him. She's going to be fine Audrey. We will help her get through this. They picked up angel and tried not to show their worry or concern for Maria. Once they were home, Mrs. Dolace got Angel settled and met her husband in the kitchen. I want her to move back home Audrey. Henry, we both want the same thing, but she's a grown woman and she has to make that decision on her own. Audrey she could have been killed! Audrey walked over to the back door and looked outside. She wanted to fall apart, but she knew she needed to keep it together. Henry walked up behind her and put his arms around her waist. He kissed her on the neck. I have prayed continuously for her safety since she left home, Audrey said. I knew that something was wrong when she stopped coming over as often as she had normally been coming. I had planned to have a talk with her, but I decided to let her work her problems out for herself. I wish I had followed my mind. Audrey, kids are going to mess up. Maria is no different from any other young adult who thinks they are so grown up. She is different Henry. She is my daughter. We did not raise her to do these things. We raised her to fear God and treat her body as a temple for

Christ. She was so upset. We did not teach her to have affairs with married men. Just thank God that this affair is over, she said. Yeah, but look what it took for it to be over. I know Henry. I know. I have so many questions to ask her Audrey. I understand why Harry wants us to put it aside, but I need answers. I have questions too Henry. You know she told me that she and Kentrel were broken up because he was seeing another woman. Yeah, the other woman was his wife Audrey. This child has been deceiving us for some time now. Yes Henry, I don't think I can believe a single word that comes out of her mouth. I have a headache Henry. I think I will try to lye down for a while. Henry watched his wife walk out of the room. He closed the back door and looked up towards the ceiling. God give us strength, he said out loud.

We all slept well that night including me.
I had wonderful thoughts instead of horrid ones
and I awoke to the sound of several voices
coming from my living room. I noticed that
Gayle had already awakened and was not in the
bed with me. I went into the bathroom to
freshen up. Then I headed for the livingroom.
I peaked my head out to see who was there. Good
morning sunshine my father said. Angel jumped
to her feet. Sister! Sister! Are you all right
now? Mama said you were sick. Are you all
right? Yes baby, I am just fine. Oh good, we
asked God to take real good care of you and to
send some angels to watch over you. Thank you
so much I said. I really appreciate it. Where
is mama? She went to church.   Maura and Jim
will drop her off after the services. I see, I
said. I've been sitting here talking to Harry

and Gayle just waiting on you to get up. I looked at Harry. She is not accustomed to giving her family too much information about her private life. Ok, I said. I think I had better get dressed, I said as I turned away from everyone.

I dressed and pouted at the same time. Why did they have to come back so soon? I am not ready for company today. I just want to be left alone. I was cross as I struggled with my clothing. I took a seat in my comfy chair and stared out of the window. I could feel that someone was watching me. I leaned up and looked around the chair. Harry was standing in the doorway watching me. Good morning, he said. Morning I said and hid myself back inside my comfy chair. I don't want to keep asking you how you are, because you won't tell me the truth. Try me, I said. Ok. How are you Maria?

Angry. Ok, lets talk about it. I don't need a

doctor Harry. I'm not here as a doctor Maria.

Now stop trying to push me away. He walked over

to the chair. He got down on his knees in front

of me. She was absolutely beautiful he thought

to himself. But he could sense the depression

she was feeling. I wouldn't even look at him.

Hello sunshine. Don't call me that. So that's

only for your dads use? I didn't answer. Why

is he here? Who your dad? Yes. Because he

loves you, and wanted to see if you were all

right. He could have called. Yes he could

have, but he didn't. Do you want me to ask him

to leave? No. That would hurt his feelings.

Well, why don't you come out and visit for a

little while and then you can come back to your

room. He touched my cheek with the back of his

fingers. I looked up at him. Ok? I took a deep breath and unfolded my legs to get out of the chair. He stood up and extended his hand to help me up. I accepted it. Maria? Yes I answered. Can I have a hug? I gave him a slight smile and leaned towards his opened arms. I definitely felt safe in his arms. He wrapped his arms around me. How does that feel to you? Fine, I said. I just want to make sure that you know that you are always safe in my arms. I know Harry. Gayle peaked her head inside the door. Excuse me you too. Mr. Dolace would like to see his daughter. Harry let go of my body and told me that he would see me when I came out. Ok, just give me a minute.

I walked out of the bedroom looking like a breath of spring flowers. I wore a turquoise ankle length straight fitting dress that complimented my figure tremendously. I put on a light sweater to cover my arms so that the bruises would be covered up. I let her hair down and the curls just bounced all over the place. I had even put on a little makeup, which took the gloomy look right off that previously occupied my face. Mrs. Dolace had arrived from church with Aunt Maura and Uncle Jim. You look beautiful honey, Mrs. Dolace said. Yes she does everyone agreed. Mr. Dolace, Harry and Uncle Jim were into a deep conversation as Harry turned to see Maria. He smiled at me and it warmed my heart to see my daddy and the man I had feelings for converse in such a manner. I could not imagine this happening with Kentrel. I smiled back at him as the eyes of her family went from one to the other. I strolled into the kitchen as I asked everyone what they wanted for breakfast. We are here to take care of you, Aunt Maura said. We don't want you to do anything for us. Now you come over here and sit down. Aunt Maura, I'm not an invalid, I am capable of fixing breakfast. Honey, do as you are told and go sit down, Aunt Maura said in an insistent tone. Aunt Maura I yelled, I was raped. There is nothing wrong with my hands. The entire room became still and there was nothing but dead silence. I'm sorry honey, Aunt Maura said as she stood before Maria with her hands opened. I took her by the hands and said, you are welcome to help me, but don't act like I can't do anything for myself. I need to get on with my life and not live in what happened a few days ago. I want all of you to hear me I said as she turned to my family. I am capable of taking care of myself, ok. Honey, we just want

to help you, Mrs. Dolace said. We know you are
capable but we just want to be here for you too,
cause we love you Maria, Gayle injected into the
conversation. I love all of you, but you have
got to let me be real about this. I was raped.
I have accepted that. He did not kill me and I
am grateful and I thank the Good Lord that there
are no other issues surrounding this except that
he stays in jail. But I have to go on with my
life. If I don't, it is just like he has taken
it away from me and he hasn't. Can you all deal
with that? Yes, Maria we can, Harry said as he
walked over to me. We want you to deal with it
too and you seem to be doing just fine. Now,
would you kindly allow us to pamper you for a
little while? But…., I tried to say. But
nothing, Harry said and maneuvered his arm
around my waist and escorted me to the living

room where the others were sitting. Mrs. Dolace
laughed out loud, finally there is somebody that
Maria can't strong arm. They all laughed out
loud. Mrs. Dolace went into the kitchen and she
and Aunt Maura cooked up a wonderful breakfast
for the family. Harry kept me close to his side
and I was becoming more accepting of his touch.
Gayle could not wait to get me alone again to
question me about Harry. She had to accept
their relationship for what she could see until
she could talk to Maria in private.

After breakfast, Maria and Harry washed the
dishes and talked as they completed the chore.
The family was preparing to leave. We will
check in on you a little later Mrs. Dolace said
as she gathered Angel up and headed for the
door. I gave hugs and kisses to my family and
saw Gayle out. Alone at last I exclaimed as I

closed the door. You are not alone, Harry exclaimed. You know what I mean, I said. No I only know what you said. Are you always this analytical, I asked? Most of the time. Well you need to lighten up. Well yes ma'am, Harry said sarcastically. I can tell you are feeling better about being around people again. What do you mean Harry? You are sounding like the lady I met a few days ago. I just smiled at him. Harry cleared his throat and starred at me. What? Maria lets talk seriously for a moment. What's wrong? You do realize that you will have to testify against Malik in court? Oh, yeah I guess. You need to do this, Maria. If for nothing else, he deserves to be put away. I know Harry. I need to be alone for a little while; I'm going to lye down. Sure, why don't you do that and I will go home for a little

while. All right I said. Harry asked if he
could take her keys so that he could let himself
in when he returned. I agreed.

CHAPTER TWELVE

I went into the bedroom and curled up in the middle of my king size bed. I lay there trying not to think about anything. But it was hopeless. The thought of Malik clouded my mind. So did being alone. I could hear everything that made a sound and even some that didn't. Even thinking about him made me feel dirty. I jumped to my feet and headed for the bathroom. The water ran over her body and she poured her favorite bath gel into the sponge to form lather. She wanted the soap and water to wash away any and every thing she felt at that moment. I will never feel clean again, I thought. *Why would Malik do this to me*, she thought? *I have never shown any type of desire for him. Why?* I sobbed as the water beat down on my face. After crying for a while and

bathing for what seemed like an eternity, I
managed to pull myself together. I put on fresh
clothes and towel dried my hair. I curled up in
the oversized chair that was close to the
window. I looked out at the world outside and
nothingness filled my soul. I felt like I had
no right to exist. I didn't see myself getting
beyond this horrible thing. I could not deal
with going to court and being made to feel like
I asked for Malik to rape me. I could only
think about the horrible things he would say to
convince people that I invited him in to have
sex. I just could not handle it. My mind
replayed the ordeal again and again. *Why did I
let him in? I should not have let him in. How
could I have known that this would happen? I
couldn't,* I thought? I began rocking back and
forth in the chair. In my mind I was saying no,

no, no. I had not heard Harry come in. He had

assumed, I was asleep and decided to just peak

in on me. He pushed the door open just a little

and did not see her in the bed. So he opened it

up all the way. He saw her in the chair rocking

back and forth. He walked over to her and

called out her name. She said no, no, no. He

got down on his knees and looked into her eyes,

but it was not Harry she saw. She continued to

say the word no. Harry grabbed both of her

shoulders and gave her a strong stiff shaking.

Maria he called out. He realized that she was

not with him. He tapped the side of her face

with his hand and called out to her again.

Maria, talk to me. Maria, I know you can hear

me. When I finally focused my eyes to his, he

could see her take a deep breath and release it.

Harry, I can't do this. Honey, do what, what

can't you do? I can't see him again. I can't

go to court Harry. I can't. I just can't. I

let him in here, don't you understand, Harry. I

let him in. Don't think about it right now,

Maria. You don't have to do anything you don't

want to, all right. It's going to be all right.

Harry wanted to soothe her but he didn't want to

lie to her. Shhh, he said don't think about

anything. I'm here now. He realized that every

time he left her alone, he came back to her in a

worse state of mind. He thought she had

progressed but now he wasn't sure. I held on to

him as if someone was trying to pull me away

from him. It's all right Maria, he continued to

say, but I was frantic. The thought of seeing

Malik made me hysterical. Harry decided to get

me a drink of white wine to help calm me down.

I could hardly hold onto the glass without

spilling the drink. Harry placed his hands
gently around mine and held the glass to my
mouth. I sipped the wine slowly. Eventually,
Harry could see that the wine was calming me
down and he released his grip on my hands.
Harry, I can't live like this anymore I said. I
can't think straight. I just can't do this
Harry. Listen, Maria, stop right now, you need
to stop honey. I want to help you but you have
to listen to me, all right? I nodded that I
was listening but I wasn't. I was thinking
about Malik and Kentrel and Malik touching me.
I want to forget Harry but it won't go away.
Harry took the glass of wine from me and placed
it on the nightstand. He turned around to face
me. Come here he said. I stood up and came to
him. He looked down at me, gazed into my eyes;
you are a very desirable woman, Maria. I don't

know what else to say to you. I don't know what else to do to make you know that you are a beautiful woman. I would love to take you in my arms and make passionate love to you. But, I know that it won't help you. I cut his word off. Make love to me. What? He said in amazement. Make love to me. Right now, I said. Maria it's not what you need. I don't know what I need Harry. I need to forget what happen. I want to put new memories in my mind. Make love to me. Are you sure that. Oh just shut up Harry I said as I reached my hand up to his face and drew him into mine, kissing him. He picked me up and sat down on the bed, placing me on his lap. I wrapped my arms around him as if I were holding on for my life. At this point I was. I want to feel good again Harry, I whispered to him. He didn't know what to say to her. Harry

wanted to make her feel good again. But he was
afraid that he would injure her state of mind
further. Not to mention hurting her physically.
Either way there would be psychological
repercussions. Maria wait, I want to talk about
this. You don't want to make love to me, I
said? I did not say that. Listen to me. I
don't want our first time to be like this. Like
what? Not like this, Maria. I just looked at
him. He held me in his arms and whispered to
me. I don't only want to be what you need baby.
I want to be what you want and desire. Can you
understand that? I nestled myself against his
chest and became quiet. It's all right he said.
Just let me hold you. I'm not going anywhere.
I promise. He knew that she did not know what
she was saying when she asked him to make love
to her. She is hanging on by a thread and she

really doesn't know what to do. She could not make love if she wanted to he thought to himself. The pain would be too much for her physically.

Some time had passed and Maria had fallen asleep in his arms. The evening was quiet and uneventful from that moment on. Her family had come to realize that she was in capable hands and were trying not to worry. It was hard for them to let her go and be an adult and now this has happened. *I am here now, he thought. I'll take care of you* Maria. His thoughts became words as he spoke them softly to her while she slept. Maria's state of mine however was another issue. He had seen these signs before and he was truly afraid. Maria was not dealing with this thing and he needed to get her into some serious therapy. I awaken to the ringing of the telephone and wondering where Harry was. I was in my bed and covered up to my waist. I got out of bed and walked over to the bedroom door. I walked out into the living room looking around. Harry was no where in sight. The television was playing on low. I walked over to the back of the sofa and there he was strecthed out and asleep. I walked around the sofa and kneeled down to him. I was smiling as I leaned over and place my lips agains his. He responded with his own lips to mine. I see you're awake, he said. Yes, I am, and I'm hungry. Are you now? Yes, and I want to go out. Where do you want to go? I feel like Sahara's. Are you sure? Yes. Well you need to change and so do I. Let me get dressed and then we can go to your place, I said. All right

It was early evening. Harry and Maria entered the resteraunt and were taken to a table. She felt good about being out again. For a little while they ate in silence, casually looking up at one another. This was a wonderful idea, Harry said as he placed his glass of wine back on the table. Yes it was, I said. It's still early, what would you like to do when we leave here. I think I would like to visit my parents. Really, you feel up to that? Yes I do. Well, parents it is. They had a nice visit with her family and was on their way home. I had spent several nights alone and made it through without incident. It was nice knowing that Harry was right down the street.

On the week after Maria was attacked, Milton met with his staff. He had several conversations with Maria's parents and Gayle

regarding her frame of mind. He wanted to put
to rest the suspicions about the attack and to
ensure that Maria's transition back to work be
as smooth as possible. Milton asked fro
everyones attention. As you know, Maria was
attacked last week. I want to ask that you not
discuss this issue with her or within this
office. I want tyou to give Maria and her
family which includes her closest friend Gayle,
all the respect that you would want if this or
any simular act were inflicted upon you or
someone you love. I will not entertain
questions about Maria or what happened to her.
I do not know exactly when she will return to
work. I do know that we all care about her and
would like to show our concern. However,
Maria's family does not feel that phone calls,
flowers or cards would be appropriate right now.

If and when she wants visitors they will let us know. For the record, I will not tolerate any harshness, ugliness or any negativity regarding this situation. Is this clear with everyone? Yes was heard around the room. Now lets get back to work, he said sternly.

CHAPTER THIRTEEN

The following weeks were uneventful for
Maria and Harry. I decided that it was time for
me to return to work. I was nervous and had
asked Gayle to ensure that people did not ask me
a lot of questions. Milton and Gayle had
handled the situation very well with my co-
workers. They promised to take care with how
they treated me. Even little miss nasty
promised to be on her best behavior. To my
surprise, they all behaved wonderfully. The day
came and went without incident. I had gathered
my things and headed down the elivator. I
stepped off the elevator and to my surprise,
there was Harry. What are you doing here? I
wanted to surprise you. And you did, I said
with a huge smile. Harry pulled me close to him
and kissed me on the lips. I hope you had a

lovely day. I did, I really did. Good. Lets
go home. As they began to walk away, Gayle
emerged from the next elevator. Hello Harry.
Hi Gayle, how are you? Just fine. I will see
you guys later I have a class tonight. See you
Gayle, they both said. As they walked to the
parking lot, Harry had taken my bag to carry it
and convienently placed his arm around my waist.
Maria, just how did you think you were getting
home today? I had not even thought about it. I
am so use to driving myself maybe I thought I
had driven to work today. Harry laughed.
What's for dinner, he said? I don't know. I
feel like eating lite. What would you like,
Harry? I would like to take my lady home and
cuddle up with her on the sofa. It might get a
little noisy. What do you mean? I mean you
stomach? They both laughed again. I tell you

what, I will drop you off and let you get
settled. Then I will pick up dinner and we
could do the cuddle thing afterwards. Sounds
like a plan. Harry dropped me off and headed
for his aprartment.

Upon entering the building he smelled a
perfume that he knew all too well. It can't be.
There she was leaning against the wall by his
door. Gina? What are you doing here? Harry ,
aren't you glad to see me? No! What in God's
name are you doing here? I had to come Harry.
You would not return my calls. I had to see
you. You need to leave. Get right back on the
plane and go home. I want to talk to you Harry.
I need you. Grow up Gina. I don't love you and
I definitely don't need you, he said with anger.
I know you are angry. Let it go, Gina, I don't
need time, I don't need space. I need you to,

so leave me alone. I will take legal aciton
again if you don't leave now. Harry that was
not called for and you know it. All I know, is
that you have got to stop this. I have moved on
with my life and you need to do the same. I
can't move on Harry, because I love you. You
didn't love me when you were cheating on me with
well lets see, Jeff, or Devin, and God knows how
many others. I know I hurt you but, you were
always so busy and I needed someone who could be
there for me. So when I'm busy, and you just
need someone again, you will just pick up the
phone and call someone else, right Gina? It's
not like that Harry. I don't have time for this
Gina. You need to leave. Harry went into his
apartment and closed the door. I do not need
this on top of the day I have had, he said as he
began undressing himself and walked into the

bathroom. I wonder if she is till out there.
What am I saying. I don't care if she is or
not. I need to clear my head. I need to keep
my mind on Maria. She needs me and God knows I
need her. I hope I got through to her this
time. When Harry came out of the shower, he
grabbed the phone book and called to order
dinner for himself and Maria. He put on his
jeans and a T-shirt and just as he finshed
tieing his shoes he heard a noise at the door.
When he opened the door, there was no one there.
He began to close the door and his eyes glimpsed
a movement from the floor. What the hell? A
baby! Hello, is anyone out here? Harry leaned
down to investigate. Hello little one. There
was a note tucked inside the car seat. It read
"Harry you didn't want to listen to me, maybe
now you will", This is your daughter, "Kaitee"

I tried to tell you on several ocassions that I was pregnant. I tried to tell you when I called you that you had a daughter. I can't handle being a parent right now. So, being that you are a more responsible person than I am, our daughter would be better off with you. Sorry it had to be this way. Love Gina". Man this is crazy. Gina! He ran out of the building and there was no one. Gina! Harry stood with his hands over his head. This is just crazy. He went back in and looked down at the baby. This is just crazy, he said again. He picked up the carrier and diaper bag and went into the apartment. He sat down on the sofa and read the note again. Gina you didn't do this to me. Damn! Kaitee started to cry. Shhh, I'm sorry, he said as he rocked the seat back and forth. What am I going to do with a baby? Harry went through the bag and found all of the babies records along with the birth certificate. Maria! He thought to himself. How in the hell will I explain this to her? I need to call her. No, my mother? Oh man? Mother is going to freak. Man I am freaking out here, he raised his voice. He was pacing the floor. Get a grip, man. Ok, Maria first then my mother. He picked up the phone and then he put it down. He picked up the diaper bag and the carrier and headed out of the door. Harry pulled up to Maria's and sat there for a moment. Ok little one, lets do this. Harry went to the door and being that he had his hands full, he pushed the door bell. I came to the door and opened it. Harry? What is this? Something you won't believe. Here take this he said as he handed me the diaper bag. They went inside and sat down on the sofa. I took the baby out of the carrier. She is precious. Harry had not said a word. He was walking back and forth. Harry? What? Whose baby is this? Surposedly mine. Yours? Harry, what are you saying? He took a deep breath. When I got home, Gina was waiting at my door. Gina? Yeah, Gina, my ex-girlfriend. We argued and I made her leave. I went in to shower and change and heard something at the door and I found this baby with a note. Did you know that she had a baby? I didn't even know she was pregnant. Man, I am not believing this. How could she do this Maria? What is going on in her head. She said it is mine, but she has fooled around on me so many times that, I can't believe this. Well, you know you will have to get the paternity test done to fine out, right? Right. She is adorable, what's her

name? The note said Kaitee. I held Kaitee so
naturally. What am I going to do with a baby?
Calm down Harry, you will upset the baby. But
Maria? Harry! Sit down. I placed Kaitee in his
arms and said just sit tight. I went through
the diaper bag and pulled out a bottle and a can
of milk and went into the kitchen. When I
returned I had a bottle ready for the baby.
When she's ready you will know it. I pulled the
other papers from the sack. Harry, she looks to
be a few months old. How old do you think she
is, he said? Let's see what these papers show.
I saw a birth certificate in there, he said.
Here it is, lets see here. Harry, Kaitee is
only 3 months old. You said you didn't know she
was pregnant. How long ago had you been
together. I had not seen Gina in over seven or
eight months. She had put on a little weight

the last time I saw her but I thought nothing of it. She was never skinny so I didn't give it any thought. She had to have been about three or four months pregnant when you saw her last, Maria said. Well, come to think of it, about three months ago, she had been leaving messages all over the place for me, but I did not want to deal with her. I just figured she was still trying to apologize for her fling with Devin Williams. You know this could not be my child, Maria. Yet, it could very well be, Harry. She doesn't even look like me. She has your eyes Harry. Maria that's not funny. She is so cute. Kaitee began to swirm in his arms. She's moving, Harry said anxiously. You men are such babies. Give her to me. I held her as if she was my own. Harry watched as I talked to Kaitee and held her like a pro. It looks so natural when women do it. Do what? Hold babies he said. That's probably why men can't have them, I said. You are probably right, Harry exclaimed with laughter. She's probably hungry. Speaking of hunger, Harry where is my dinner. Oh no, the restaurant. I will be back in a flash. He jumped to his feet and out of the door. As I sat holding Kaitee, I looked over the birth certificate. Mother "Ginarette Montgomery", Father " Harry Stonewell". Well I'll be. Could he be lying? How could his name be on the birth certificate without his signature? I was concerned. Her train of thought was interrupted by the ringing of the phone. Hello? Hi honey, how are you? Fine mama, how are you? Just great. How was your first day back to work? It went well. You don't sound like yourself. What's wrong? I can't get into to it right this moment mama, but I will talk to you about it for sure a little later. Are you sure? Do you need me to come over? No I don't. I am sure of it. Where is Harry? He went to pick up dinner. You are eating kind of late aren't you. Well, something came up and he was running late. Well you call me when you are ready to talk ok? I sure will, I love you mama. I love you too baby. Good night. Good night mama. Just then Harry walked in. I'm back. Harry what are we going to do with the baby tomorrow? We both have to work. I can get mama to come over and watch her or we can drop her off to her. Mama! I need to call my mother. I don't want to involve her until I find out for sure that Kaitee is mine. Well, we need to take a ride to my parents house, don't you think, I said. In the mean time I am going to call Dr. Michaels to set up the test for tomorrow. I think I can rearrange my schedule for tomorrow. But I would like to talk to your folks. After they had their meal, they gathered up Kaitee and headed for Maria's parents. It was about a thirty minute ride across town and they finally arrived. I hope they haven't gone to bed. No, dad is watching tv and mama is cleaning the kitchen. It is a ritual around here. They rang the door bell and waited for someone to come to the door. Mr. Dolace opened the door. Maria what are you doing here so late? What's wrong? Sorry for coming by so late dad, but we needed to talk to you. Come on in. Good evening sir, how are you? Fine, what in the world do you have here. Kaitee began to cry as they entered the house. Well this is what we want to talk to you about, I said. Mrs. Dolace came out of the

kitchen, my Lord, what are you doing here? A
baby! Whose baby is this Mrs. Dolace asked?
Well, we think it's Harrys'. Harry! They both
said in unisom. For the love of Jobe, come in a
sit down. Mama, daddy, this is Kaitee. She was
left at Harry's door this evening, by his ex-
girlfriend. I see, go on, Mr. Dolace said. Did
you know anything about this little bundle son?
No sir, this is all news to me. I see. Let me
get a look at this litle beauty, Mrs. Dolace
said. She lifted the baby for the seat. Hello
pudding. You are a tiny little angel aren't
you. What's going on in here Angel said as she
walked out of the hall way rubbing her eyes?
Maria! Maria! She said as she focused her eyes.
Hello sweetpea. Hows my little angel girl? I'm
ok. A baby! A baby! We have a baby. Let me
see mama, let me see. Calm down Angel, you will

frighten her with all of that noise. This is

Kaitee. Hello Kaitee. Mama she is pretty. Is

she ours? Can we keep her? Angel calm down.

Mrs. Dolace, I need someone to watch her for me

during the day. I don't want to get my mother

involved until I am sure of paternity. Where is

the mother of this baby Mr. Dolace asked? We

don't know. Gina left her with a note and took

off. Mama, Harry's name is on the birth

certificate. Son, I thought you said you did

not know about the baby. I don't, I mean I

didn't. I honestly don't know how or who signed

the papers. But for sure it wasn't me. I never

knew of this child until this evening. I never

knew that Gina was ever pregnant until today. I

am asking if you will care for her during the

day while we are at work until I can make other

arrangements. We? I don't like that you are

involved in this Maria, Mr. Dolace said. Daddy
I am perfectly all right. You all have to get
on with your lives and let me put this behind
me. Sometimes a new focus is a good thing.
Even if it comes in the form of a little
blessing like Kaitee. I think I need a little
diversion from what I've been dealing with.
Harry is apart of my life and whatever affects
him affects me. So yes, we are going to take
care of Kaitee. Harry took care of me when I
needed him and I will be there when he needs me.
Harry has set up paternity test for tomorrow and
we will bring Kaitee over after the test is
done. If it's all right with you? Yes honey I
will care for her, Mrs. Dolace said. You forget
that she is your daughter and she is head strong
just like you, said Mrs. Dolace to her husband.
I will pay you what ever you ask. That is not

necessary son, you are apart of our family.
Thank you so much. Well we must go and try to
get settled. Whose keeping the baby tonight,
Mr. Dolace asked? We both are, I said. Don't
tell me you have moved in together, Mrs. Dolace
questioned? No mama, Harry doesn't know the
first thing about babies. Could you just
imagine him during the night. Calling me
because he don't know what to do. So why even
go through that. When I can just be there.
Lord help us, Mrs. Dolace said. It's all right
Mr. and Mrs. Dolace. I have the greatest
respect for your daughter and the both of you.
I would not compromise her virtue in any way. I
promise. We appreciate your honesty son. Good
night. Good night everyone I said as I picked
up the baby and kissed my parents and Angel. I
will see you on tomorrow.

When we made it to the car, I looked at

Harry. So, you will not compromise my virtue.

No siree, he said. I promised your parents and

a man's word is his bond. I smiled and focused

my attention on the baby. So, where are we

sleeping tonight, I asked him? You have the

bigger bed, so I guess we will stay at your

place. We need to get a baby bed and some other

necessities. Like what, he asked? Diapers,

formula, clothes, you know the necessities. You

are really clueless when it comes to kids aren't

you? I have never had the need to know these

things Maria. I have only dealt with adults.

Well Dr. Stonewell, it is time for you to be

clued in. Tomorrow we go shopping. Bring your

check book and credit cards. Wait Maria, this

kid could not be mine and I don't intend on

spending a fortune on someone that may not be

around to enjoy it. Harry Stonewell how could
you think like that? I'm thinking rationally.
You on the other hand are thinking with your
maternal instincts. But I like that he said. I
felt something I had not felt in along time. I
felt loved. Quietness filled the vehicle. My
hand was covered by his as I held onto the
carrier.

CHAPTER FOURTEEN

Once we returned home, I washed what
clothing the baby had, filled the other bottles
with formula. I felt Harry's eyes on me and I
turned to catch him watching me. What? You are
amazing. Why? I don't know. I just can't get
over how you can go from needing to be taken
care of, to taking care of someone else. She
needs us Harry. What ever my problem is right
now, Kaitee's is much larger. She can't do for
herself, and it is up to us to do for her.
Don't you feel that in your heart. Don't you
feel that she needs you just the way you felt
that I needed you? Yes, but I don't know what
to do for her. I know how to help you. But how
do I help her? You just love her Harry. Hold
her and love her, the way you held me. He
brushed my hair away from my face and tilted my

chin up and kissed me gently on the lips. Watch
it, this could be dangerous. I'll take my
chances, he said. He kissed me deeply this time
and I returned his kiss. When he released my
lips, he sighed yes this feels so right. I know
it is right. I just listened. You must be
tired, he said. Yes I am. Well, go on and get
ready for bed. I will let you ladies have the
bed and I will sleep on the sofa. Oh no you
won't. If we have to all sleep on the floor we
will all be together. Ok, so what do you want
to do, he asked? Come on lets make a pallet on
the floor. That way we can all be comfortable.
While they made a place for the baby and then
one for themselves, Harry gave her some news she
had been waiting for. I got the results from
the lab work at the hospital. What are you
talking about? I had forgotten all about the

test they were going to run at the hospital
after the rape.   Remember in the ER they took
blood to run test along with the sample of
fluids they took? Oh yes, I remember now.
Well, I picked them up and every thing is fine.
They did not find anything wrong. We had taken
our place on the comforter that was spreed out
for us to sleep on. I was quiet. Maria? Just
hold me Harry. It felt good lying in Harry's
arms. Fear tried to creep in several times.
But I had to tell myself over and over that it
is safe in Harry's arms. Maybe it was actually
being on the floor with Harry that made me so
uncomfortable. Or maybe it was hearing the news
and drumming up old ghost. He looked into my
eyes and caressed my face with his fingers.
Something is wrong, he said as he watch my face.
It's nothing. Maria, there is nothing in this

world you can't say to me. I want to know what's on your mind. Am I doing something that upsets you? No, I don't think so. I don't know, it feels so uncomfortable bieng like this with you. Would it upset you if I talked about what happened to you? I got quiet. One thing that I found helps rape victims a lot is talking about what happened. A persons biggest problem is holding everything in. This is not something that you can wish away. It happened and you have a choice. You can get it out into the open or you can hide behind it. There are consequences behind both. I continued to listened. He continued. Talking about what happened gets all the demons out. There is nothing left to hide behind. I want to help you sweetie. Lets face the demon. Let's face it together. He set up and leaned his back against the bed. Come here and sit with me. I crawled over to him. Sit right here, I want to hold you. I want you to get use to my touch. I want you to get use to me holding you. As long as you know the safty of these arms and my touch you will be fine. Nervousness was welling up from the pit of my stomach. He spread his legs and I sat between them with my back to him. Now, he said. All I want you to do is breath. Let your body relax next to mine. I eased my back against his chest and took a deep breath. He could feel my tention. Can you feel my breathing pattern? Yes, I said. Good, just relax and pay attention to the rhythm. He took my right hand in his and gently stroked my hand and then my fingers. To my surprise, it was very relaxing. That feels good I told him. Um hm, he said. If you are relaxed now, maybe we had better get some sleep, before the baby wakes up. Harry? Yes? I'm sorry that you are not comfortable with making love to me. If I had no been raped would you have felt the same way? Maria, I am not uncomfortable with making love to you. I just know that its not what you need right now. I can decide that for myself Harry. I don't need someone to dictate when I should or should not have sex. Maria, don't ever make the mistake of thinking that we will ever have sex. I have fallen in love with you and I will make love to you. Have sex with you, no sweetness, I will never have sex with you. There is a difference and one day I plan to show you what making love is all about. I'll be waiting Harry. Good night sweetness, good night Harry.

The nights slumber was broken with Kaitee's crying. I was up and warming the bottle when

Harry heard the cry from the other room. It's all right, he heard me say. He stood in the door way watching me as I bounced the baby on my shoulder. Yeah, I bet you are hungry aren't you. Well, just a few more minutes and you will be just fine. How long have you two been up? Good morning sleepy head, I turned and said to him. We've been up a little while. He walked over to me and kissed me on the cheek. Good morning. Harry? Yes? You did not kiss your daughter. Maria, lets not go there. Harry, babies can feel when they are not wanted. Don't ever do that again ok. Harry took Kaitee from me arms and said hello Kaitee. I didn't mean to hurt your feelings. I'm just not use to being affectionate with kids. You forgive me don't you Kaitee? Kaitee gurgled with her fingers in her mouth. See she forgives me. What about

you? Give her to me, and go brush your teeth.
Are you trying to tell me something? Yes in a
nice and pleasant way, go brush. All right,
I'll go. I finshed preparing the baby's bottle
and was feeding her when he returned. Have you
eaten? Not yet. What would you like? Just
toast and Juice. I think you need a little bit
more than that, sweetie. We don't have time.
Yes we do, he said. You have to make time, even
if you have to be late for something else. I
want you to stay healthy. What are you talking
about? I am talking about you becoming Mrs.
Harry Stonewell. Harry stop it. Maria? She
looked up from the baby, yes? I have given this
plenty of thought and I. He paused. I would
like, I mean, Maria will you marry me? Harry we
have known each other a little less than four
months. I don't need to have known you for

several years or months to know that I want and

need you in my life, for the rest of my life.

Harry you might decide tomorrow that you hate

me. I could never hate you baby. Stop making

excuses and answer the question. Could I at

least think about it? No. I love you, he said

so softly that I could have cried. I fell in

love with you the first time I saw you. My love

for you has grown since I met you. I know that

you feel something for me Maria. Do you love

me? Harry that isn't fair. You have had time

to think about it. Why shouldn't I? All

right, you can think about it. Nothing you can

say will change how I feel about you. Just

remember how I feel about you while you are

thinking about it. I smiled at him. In an

attempt to change the subject, I asked, what

time are you taking Kaitee for blood work this

morning? I don't know, I'll call Dr. Michaels
and then I will let you know. Good, I want to
be there. You know you don't have to. Yes I
know, but I want to. Well, we will just have to
pick you up. It's time for me to get dressed
and get out of here I said. Not before
breakfast. You have your rules and I have mine.
Go on and get dress and I will finish up in
here. Kaitee has to be burped. I will handle
it. You don't even know how. It can't be too
hard and I have seen it done. Just tell me what
to do. Put this on your shoulder. Ok he said.
Now put her on you shoulder but not too high.
Then you need to gently pat her on the back
until she burps. Make little small circles like
this. Ok,I got it. I'll be back in a flash.

When Maria returned she was just gorgeous.
She actually glowed. The indigo pants suit fit

her like it was tailor made for her figure. The silver necklace and matching earrings complimented the buttons on her jacket. As usual her hair was flawless. She didn't have time to apply makeup, so she carried a small bag in her hand. Simply gorgeours he said. Thank you. Kaitee was in the carrier, making all sorts of sounds which could only mean one thing, she had a stinky diaper. Come on daddy lets get a little more experience. What now? The changing of the diaper. Oh God. You can do it daddy. Don't call me that. Harry you will have to get a grip on this. You could very well be her father. Until I know, I don't want you to use that terminology on me. All right. How long will it take to get the results? Dr. Michaels is a good friend of mine and he will put a rush on it. I'll never get use to doing

this, he said. Yes you will. If we get
married…. When we get married you mean he said
quickly. Ok right, when we get married, we will
have babies and you will do this. Well I will
have to deal with it then. There you go little
missy, all done. Go to your dad, I'm sorry.
Here you go Harry. I need to get my breakfast
and be on my way. Have a good day he said. She
will need another bottle in about two to three
hours. She will let you know. Good luck. She
was out the door. Well, little lady, what am I
going to do with you this morning? Kaitee made
a few little faces at him and he had to laugh.
You are too cute, but don't tell Maria I said
so.

When I arrived at work I went in to let
Milton know that I had an important apointment
to attend to and that I would be back as soon as

I could. He didn't have a problem with it.   I
had confided in Gayle and asked her not to say
anything to anyone. I also told her that Harry
asked me to marry him this morning. Gayle
wanted to scream. Shhh, I said as I closed the
door to my office. Gayle jumped up and hugged
me so tightly. Hold on girl, I didn't say yes.
Are you crazy? The man is crazy in love with
you. What is the problem? I don't know Gayle.
Don't you think that it is too soon? Look, Ron
and I were off and on throughout our entire
relationship. Now we are getting married on
Valentines Day. I can't wait to be his wife.
Maria this is it girl. You have been waiting on
a man like Harry all of your life. I know it
cause you have told me millions of times. You
have to do this. Do it girl. Say yes. I
smiled. I do love him, Gayle. I'm just afraid.

Afraid of what? Gayle I don't even know if I can handle being with a man since I was raped. At least you can say it now Maria. Thanks to Harry and Dr. Helen, I have made great progress in winning the war over this thing. You have done a wonderful job in putting it behind you Maria. Don't let him win. If you don't accept this proposal you will regret it the rest of your life. Harry needs you as much as you need him. Tell me I'm lieing Gayle said. I know you're not. I don't know, I said again. I have gone through so much. You know, sometimes I feel like I don't deserve to be happy. God is not like that Maria and you know it. That's just you having a pitty party. I'm your best friend and I can't lie to you. I never liked what you were doing with Kentrel and I have expressed my opinion on that subject many times.

But, Maria you and Harry are so right for each other. He adores you and well I don't need to tell you how you feel about him. I see the way you two look at each other. If that isn't love then tell me what is? I know you are right girl. My parents will say it's too soon. Did Harry ask your parents to marry him? No silly. Then why are you going there? Look, for the first time in your life do what is right for Maria. The phone buzzed in as they laughed. Childs/Anderson, Maria speaking. Hi Maria, it's Carlan. Hey how are you? Fine and you? Good, what can I do for you? We are planning a meeting to finalize the family reunion and I wanted to see if you would be free this weekend. Which day? Saturday around 4:30. I don't have anything to do that I know of, where are we meeting? Your place. They both laughed. Well,

that's fine. My place and you all bring the
snacks. Good enough, see you then. Ok Carlan.
What's going on, Gayle asked? Family reunion
meeting, I forgot all about the reunion. You
sure you want to handle this, your plate's been
pretty full lately. I know, but if I backed out
they would ask more questions. So lets just get
it over with. You have always been so strong
Maria and I've admired that about you. Thanks
Gayle now we had better get back to work before
we are both looking for jobs. See you later.
Oh don't for get you need to go for a fitting
for my wedding in about three weeks. Put it on
your planner. Ok. See you later.

Meanwhile Harry called Dr. Michaels and he
was ready for him to bring the baby in. He
immediately called Maria to meet them outside
the building in the next thirty minutes. The

test did not take very long and Maria consoled Kaitee as Harry had his blood drawn. Then they were off. We can't go shopping this evening. Maria you have therapy this evening. You can't skip this. Harry it's just one meeting. Maria it is very important that you keep your appointments. We can shop anytime. You are going and that is all to it. Don't tell me what to do Harry. I love you Maria. I only want what is good for you. You need this. You need it, trust me will you. I'll pick up Kaitee and then I'll meet you at your place after your session with Helen. We can shop then. I wasn't taking kindly to being bossed around. Harry sinced it.

Harry dropped me back at work and went on with the baby. After work I drove to my session. During my session with Helen I realized that I still had a long way to go to get through my pain. Helen made her notes to my file regarding my progress. Maria this is only to help you she said. I know that you need to get some things out of your system. I need you to do something for me. What? I need you to start writing things down for me. On your next session, I want you to bring in this journal. I want you to record what you are feeling and when you feel these feelings. What will this accomplish? Just do it and you will understand on your next session. I will see what I can do.

CHAPTER SIXTEEN

I made my way home and had expected to see Harry and Kaitee there. No one was home. I called my parents house to see if Harry had picked up the baby. Hello, Dolace residence. Harry? Hey sweetie, how was your session? Harry, what are you still doing there? Your mother wanted to give Kaitee a bath before we left. Matter of fact I am on my way to pick you up. She is going to keep Kaitee while we shop. Be ready in about twenty minutes. Harry it takes thirty minutes to come for across town. You just need to know how to drive, see you soon. I changed out of my work attire and was sipping on a cup of tea when Harry arrived. Hello beautiful. Hello. You know if anyone would have told me I would be this happy, I would have told them they were lying, he said.

Are you ready to go? What has come over you Mr.
Stonewell? I don't know, I just feel so good
tonight. Harry whisked me up from my seat and
pulled me close to him. I told your parents
that I asked you to marry me. Why did you do
that? Why must you inform my family of every
thing that goes on between us? I moved out so
that I can be on my own and be independent of
them. Harry you have to stop this. I'm sorry,
I wasn't thinking. I was just so happy that I
just lost my head. Baby believe me, if I knew
that it would have upset you this way, I would
not have told them anything. I truly am sorry.
I just feel over whelmed Harry. I need some
air. I went to the door and opened it and came
face to face with Malik. I screamed and time
stood still. Maria, I just wanted to talk to
you he said. I know I should not be here. You

bastard, Harry yelled. I stood in the doorway
paralized with fear. Harry grabbed me by the
arm and pulled me away. You no good bastard,
how dare you come back here. Before he knew it
he hit Malik in the face and knocked him out
cold. Give me the phone. Harry called 911.
The police didn't take long to arrive. They
arrested Malik for breaking the restraining
order that was issued against him after the
rape. I just wanted to talk to her, he said. I
wasn't going to hurt her. Just get him out of
here, before I hit him again. Harry turned his
attention to Maria, who was sitting on the sofa
shaking and still in a state of shock. Maria?
Harry, he said that he was coming back. Honey
he is gone. The police has him now. He is
going back to jail. But they let him out,
Harry. He is going to get me again. Harry, I

have to get out of here, I have to get out of here. I was screaming again. Harry had to physically hold me down. I had completely freaked out. I began to hyperventalate. There was a knock on the door. Come in Harry yelled. It was one of the police officers. Get the paramedics quick. The officer responded quickly to Harry's demand. He was trying to help Maria as best he could. Breathe honey, come on. Lossen up your grip and try to relax. I need you to listen to the sound of my voice. Breathe honey that's it, take your time, listen to my voice, good girl. I'm here with you and no one can hurt you. I've got you now. Everything is all right. The paramedics arrived and was giving me oxygen and under Harry's instructions they had given me something to calm me down. Dr. Stonewell, would you like her transported to

the Medical Center. Yes. I will accompany you.
Don't leave me Harry, I said in despiration.
I'll never leave you Maria. I'll be right here.

Once I was checked out at the hospital,
Harry decided that he wanted me to stay
overnight and that he wanted me to be watched.
I am fine now Harry, I want to go home. Home
Maria, you could not stand being in that
apartment for another second. You completely
freaked out. Now you are telling me that you
want to go back to the place that you could not
wait to get out of. Well, I will go to your
place. I just need to get out of this hospital.
I know that you feel that way right now, but you
need the rest. You will not rest if you go home
tonight. I will handle everything else. Oh no,
the baby, she said. I will handle the baby.
Harry you can't take care of her like I can. I

need to get the baby and take care of her.
Maria, stop and listen to me. I have asked them
to give you something to help you sleep. It
will soon take affect. You will get some rest
if I have to stay here with you all night. What
about the baby? Your parents can handle her for
the night. I'll call them. I promise. I will
stay here with you, all right. All right Harry.
She had gotten drowsy. Good girl. The
medication is beginning to work. Get some sleep
honey. Sure Harry.

Harry walked outside the room and down the
hall to the nurses station. He picked up the
phone, when Dr. Michaels walked up to him. What
are you doing here? We had a little problem and
I brought Maria in. Is she all right? She will
be fine. We are just keeping her here to get
some rest and to just watch her through the

night. I heard about what happened to her.
Yeah, the jerk had the nerve to come back
tonight. You have got be kidding Harry. Man I
think I broke my fingers I hit him so hard. Let
me look at that hand. You are swelling, you
need to get this X-rayed. Nurse? Yes doctor.
See that Dr. Stonewell get this hand X-rayed
asap. Yes doctor. Looks like you're the
patient tonight doc. I want those sent up to me
stat. Yes doctor the nurse responded. Come on
Dr. Stonewell, let's get that x-ray done. Harry
turned and told the other nurse to keep an eye
on Maria.

When Harry returned he had a cast on his
hand. He picked up the phone and dialed the
Dolace's. Hello Dolace residence. Hello Mr.
Dolace, I am sorry we are late picking up the
baby. We had a little trouble. What happened,

Harry is Maria all right? Malik showed up to the apartment. Is Maria ok? I brought her to the hospital. Jesus, we are on our way. No wait. Just listen, she's fine. He didn' get a chance to touch her. I made sure of it. She just freaked out from seeing him. I asked them to keep her overnight. She's been given a seditive and she will probably sleep through the night. Harry you are a good man. Thank you for bieng there. So what happened? Well, we sort of got into it about me tell you that I asked her to marry me. She opened the door to walk out and there he was. After I hit him and knocked him out, I called the police and then she just flipped out. She was having trouble breathing so I had he police call the paramedic and we are here. I am so glad that you were there. How did that punk get out of jail Mr.

Dolace asked? I am sure he had someone bail him out. I don't think he will be so lucky this time. I will make sure of it. Well, if you don't mind, would you keep Kaitee overnight and we will see you tomorrow. Thanks son, I appreciate you being there for my little girl. I love her Mr. Dolace and I would not be anywhere else. Good night son. Good night sir. The nurse was smiling at him as he hung up the phone. You are something else she said. Naw, just a man in love. Yes you are. I'll be in Ms. Dolace's room if I'm needed. Mr. Dolace informed his wife of what was going on. She remembered Maria telling her about the family reunion meeting tomorrow. She called Carlan and canceled the meeting for her. Carlan wanted to know why Maria was canceling the meeting. She's not feeling well right now Carlan, and as soon

as she can talk to you she will call. Thanks
Auntee Audrey for calling me. It's not a
problem Carlan. Once they hung up, Carlan could
tell that something was really wrong. Maura had
told her about Maria being raped and she asked
her not to talk about it. She had honored her
wish. But now she was worried about her cousin.
I will wait to hear from her later this week,
she thought.

When I awakened the next morning, I saw
Harry's hand in a cast. Harry, your hand, what
happened? Good morning sunshine. Your hand
Harry, what happened to your hand? Well your
memory may be a little foggy but mine isn't.
Your visitor yesterday made me the recipient of
a few broken fingers. My hands went over my
face as I said his name. "Malik". When will
this madness stop? When you testify at his

trial and send him to jail for a good long time. I understand that now. The door opened and Dr. Michaels entered the room. Good morning. Hello Dr. Michaels. How are you feeling today? I guess I am all right. We were just recalling the events of yesterday. Well, I have your release papers signed and you can leave whenever you are ready. You on the other hand, I want to see you in a week to check this hand out. I understand from the xrays that it is fractured and you may need pins. Yes. I will have to look at it next week and make a decision then. All right, lets get you out of here. Harry told me to stay put and he would go and get the truck. Once he picked me up and we were on our way, I glanced at him every once in a while. I could see that he had a very unusual look on his face. Are you all right Harry? I'm working through it. What do you mean? I just want to

know if you are all right? Just like you,

Maria, I want this to be over. I want Malik out

of our lives. He hadn't notice that he was

being stern. I remained quiet for the duration

of the ride. Harry was feeling hard press with

his own problems. He knew he needed to pick up

the baby and give the Dolaces their daugheter.

What a trade off. Both of them were problems to

him right now. He felt that he need some time

away for both of them. But how would he be able

to say that to Maria. Once they made it to

Maria's parents house, he just sat in the truck

for a few minutes. Harry, what is happening

here? It will all work out Maria. Let's just

go inside ok. I opened my door. Just wait I'll

help you down. But I didn't wait for him. I

stepped down from the truck, closed the door and

walked away. Mrs. Dolace was holding Kaitee as she opened the door to let them in. Oh my Lord, Harry, what happened to your hand. I broke I when I hit that no good creep. If you don't mind could I leave the girls in your care for a little while. I really need to take care of something. Sure, Mrs. Dolace said. Harry turned and walked back to his truck, got in and drove away. Mrs. Dolace turned her attention to her daughter. Are you all right? She placed the baby in the little bed she had Henry pull from the attic. I began to cry as my mother tried to find out what happened. I think that this is all too much for him. Mama I don't know what to do. He is so angry right now. I just don't know what to do. I want to be what he needs but he just won't let me. I don't know what else to do. Honey, be yourself. If it is

not enough for him then you can't change it.
Trust him baby, Mrs. Dolace said. I need to
call my office. I'll be in the kitchen.

I called for Milton and was put on hold.
While I waited, I tried to fix my mind and
words. Dawson speaking. Milton this is Maria.
Hello Maria, what's up? Milton I hate to do
this to you right now. Do what Maria? Maria
took a deep breath. I need to take a leave of
absence. I thought everything was going well.
Milton he came back, I said as my voice began to
tremble. Calm down where are you? I am at my
parents' house. I was just released from the
hospital this morning. Oh Maria, I'm so sorry.
As tears ran down my face, I explained the
events of yesterday to him. I can't think
straight Milton. I have been seeing a counselor
since this happened and right now I can't even

say if it is helping me. I am a complete wreck right now and I couldn't do you any good being at work. That's quite all right Maria. You are a good employee and I will do everything I can to preserve your position here. Let me check into a few things and I will get back with you. Where will you be? At my house or my parents' house. Great, you just do what ever it takes to get yourself together and I will handle things on this end. Thanks Milton, I really appreciate your help. Tell Gayle I will call her later. Thanks again.

I walked outside the back door and sat in the swing. I wanted to cry and yet I wanted to be strong. It was hard to be either of the two at that moment. When I was troubled my mother use to always come with a scroungy and finger comb my curly locks of hair and then pull them

together through the scrungie. Just then the
door opened and there she was with her scrungie
on her arm. She stood behind me and fingered
through my hair. I knew you would come. I had
to, because you are still my little girl. Even
if you want to feel all grown up and try to be
all grown up, you will always be my little girl.
Thanks mama. You are welcome. Come on inside
and get some breakfast.

CHAPTER EIGHTEEN

Harry went home to shower and change. He then went to see his lawyer. He had several items on his agenda. First he spoke to him concerning the baby and Gina. Once they finished he then spoke to him concerning the issue of Maria and Malik. Thompson was a prominent attorney in the area and he was good at what he did. He picked up the phone and made a few calls while Harry sat and waited. When he finished, he looked up at Harry and said, "We will make sure he stays in jail for a long time". Will she have to go to court? Probably, but I will see what I can do. Good. Well Tommy, as usual you are the man. I know and the bill is all yours. So is the check, thanks for everything he told him. I will get the test results to you as soon as they are in Harry said as he reached for the door.

Harry went to his office and did a letter to the administrator to take a little more time to get himself settled. He then went to see his mother. Ms. Sara was happy to see her son. Hello mama. Harry where have you been? I been worried that you are working too much. Mama there is so much that I need to tell you. Harry explained to her about his feelings for Maria. Then he told her about Kaitee. She was understanding, but angry that he felt he could not come to her. I just did not want to burden you with my problems. You are my son and your problems are mine. If I am a grandmother, I want to know about it. I understand about Maria. You can bring her by anytime. I want to see my new daughter-in-law to be. Mama, she is

going through a lot. So it will just take some
time. I am hoping that having the baby around
will help move the memory of the rape. But time
will tell. Now I have to be going. I will call
you later. I love you son, and I love you mama.

Harry made one more stop. It was to his
favorite jeweler. He browsed the cabinet for a
while and then he asked for the manager. Well
as I live and breathe. Harry Stonewell is that
you? Yes sir, Mr. Chandler. Son, how are you?
I will be fine once I find what I'm looking for.
Well come on to the back and let's see if we
have what you need. Mr. Chandler had a small
selection for his special customers. He opened
a cabinet and pulled out a beautiful wooden box.
There were two trays of gorgeous rings. Take
your time and let me know if you see anything.

He left Harry to the box because he knew that he could afford the entire box if he wanted it.

Harry looked through the trays carefully and there in the center of the second tray was the most beautiful ring he had ever seen. Mr. Chandler? You called? Yes sir, I found what I am looking for. Oh yeah that one is beautiful. How long will it take to size it? What size do you need? I believe a five. Well we can just clean it up and box it up. Are you serious? Yep. Don't you want to know how much it is? No. It doesn't matter. I'll take it. Well, how do you want to pay? Bill me. I'll call the bank and have the check sent right over. Let me have Janice clean it up and get you a box. Harry was grinning from ear to ear. Lucky girl, Janice said. No, I'm the lucky one.

Harry pulled up to the Dolaces, and sat there for a little while. I came to the door and watched him. I walked out to the truck and got in on the passenger side. I sat there beside him. He reached out and took my hand. I'm sorry for the fowl mood earlier. I'm sorry if I caused it I said. No, it's not your fault sweetness. I wish you would stop saying that Harry. It is my fault. If it weren't for me, you would not be going trough these emotional trips. Maria, I need to take fault for some of what has taken place today. I drove away and left you and Kaitee here without explanation. You see I know who I am and what I want. You may think that my actions are crazy, but I am as sure of what I am about to do than I am about breathing. I meant what I said when I told you I was falling in love with you. I do love you.

If you are not ready for that I can understand.
I will wait until you are. Harry, listen, she
tried to interrupt him. No, you listen. I
don't know if Katiee is mine. It feels as if
she is as far as feelings go. I have put
everything in motion to find out if she is and
if she is not, well, I want to adopt her. I was
surprised by what he was saying. Now, about
you. I know that its only been months since
that terrible ordeal with Malik. I know that
you still have a lot to work through mentally
and physically. As long as I can hold you in my
arms and you know that I love you, I am willing
to wait for the rest to happen. I want you to
know that I don't plan on going anywhere. Oh
Harry, I said as the tears ran down my face. He
lifted my face and kissed me gently on the lips.
You see Maria. I feel you here in my heart.

When you hurt, so do I. When you're happy, I
feel it. You are connected to my soul and I
don't ever want that feeling to end. Never!
Tears began to run even more as he spoke those
loving words to me. Well, I think you have
taken enough time to think about my question.
He reached into his jacket pocket and pulled out
a beautiful navy blue box. He placed the box in
the hand with the cast on it. He took his other
hand to pick up my left hand and looked into my
eyes. Maria Dolace, I love you and I want to
spend the rest of my life with you. He turned
my hand over with the palm facing upward. He
then reaches over with the cast hand and placed
the box in the palm of my hand and closes it
over the box with both of his hands. He held on
to my hand and the box and sighed. Let me ask
you again. Maria wiped her eyes with the other

hand. Harry, what is this? Open it, he said.
I pulled my hand from his. I opened the box and
inside I found the most precious diamond ring.
I sat there as more tears streamed down my face
and one hand covering my mouth. Mr. and Mrs.
Dolace watched from the window. Harry took the
ring from the box and asked me again. Maria
Dolace, will you make me the happiest man in the
world? Will you marry me? Yes Harry, Yes!
Harry placed the ring on my finger and took me
in his arms and kissed me deeply. Mrs. Dolace
had tears in her eyes and Mr. Dolace had to pull
her away from the window to give us some
privacy. Harry noticed them in the window, but
Maria did not. I was filled with so much
emotion that I could not stop crying. I hope
these are happy tears, Harry asked? They are
happy aren't they? Yes, I said, very happy.

Wait right here. Harry got out of the truck and went around to the other side. I guess you will allow me help you out of the vehicle this time? Yes. I see that you are full of yes's today, also. Yes I am. Harry helped me out of the truck and took me in his arms and kissed me again. Thank you, he said as he took his lips from mine. As we walked into the house, Harry yelled, she said yes! Congratulations honey, I am happy for the both of you, Mrs. Dolace said. Welcome to the family son, Mr. Dolace said. Thank you sir. You can drop the sir Harry. You can call me dad. Thanks dad. This is a wonderful day for me, Harry said as he ran his hands through me hair. Well, I think I had better get these girls home. Harry we still need to pick up some things for the baby. Honey we have plenty of time to do that. Look, why don't you two let us keep Kaitee here and you two can just spend the day together. We can take care of her. Are you sure? We love having her here. We will check in a little later all right, Harry said. That's fine, don't rush back, Mrs. Dolace said as she ushered them out of the door. We walked out of the house hand in hand. Harry opened the door and helped me in, then he walked around to the drivers side. He felt like he was floating on air.

Harry and I went to my apartment so that I could shower and change. Harry was on clouds while he waited for me. He laid across the bed, looking up at the ceiling. I have a lot to be thankful for. I was in the shower feeling some of those same feelings. I was humming a tune I had heard on the radio earlier. Do I have to come in there to get you? You might, I replied.

Are you afraid to come get me? Sweetie, I am

not afraid. I am careful, there is a difference

you know. Just then, Harry heard the water stop

and Maria's beautiful face peered around the

door of the bathroom. Did you miss me? I

always do, sunshine. She wrapped herself in a

beautiful lavender sheet towel. Her curly hair

fell around her glowing face. She did not look

like someone who had just spent the night in the

hospital from a frightening encounter with the

man who had raped her. I want to give you the

world Maria Dolace. I have the world Harry, as

long as you are in it. They stared into each

other's eyes. Harry held her close to him as

his thoughts took him to places he could only

dream of right now. His mind was drenched by

her aroma and it made him drunk with desire for

her. He had promised to do right by her and

that meant giving her all the respect she deserved. Without making her feel undesired, he whisked her around and pointed her to the closet. You had better get yourself dressed if we are going to have a baby bed for Kaitee tonight. Not to mention clothes and formula, I added. I am going to get something to drink and you sunshine should be ready in about fifteen minutes. Harry walked out of the room and turned on the television. I am the luckiest man in the world. Maria walked out of the room looking radiantly beautiful. There was a calm about her. She felt the life come back to her. She had purpose again.

CHAPTER NINETEEN

After a few days had gone by Harry received a call about the paternity test. He wanted to go alone to Dr. Michaels to hear the results of the test. What are you afraid of Harry? You said that even if she is not yours that you wanted to keep her. So what is the problem? I don't know, I just feel like going alone. Are we a family Harry? Yes, Maria, what makes you ask that question? The fact that you want to exclude us from hearing the results. I'm sorry baby. I am so glad that I have you. He wrapped his arms around me. You forgive me? Yes, just don't do it again I said as I kissed him. Ok, I wont. Good. Let me get Kaitee and we can leave. Kaitee was taking a nap in the bedroom. I gathered the daiper bag and pulled a few bottles from the refridgerator. I picked Kaitee up and put her in the carrier. We are ready, I said. Harry picked up the carrier and headed for the door. What vehicle are we taking? We can go in my car. Harry buckled Kaitee's seat into the backseat and closed the door. I was buckling my seatbelt and waiting for Harry to get in on the drivers side. It's been so long since I drove a car he said. We drove in silence for a few minutes. Are you nervous Harry? Yes, I have never been through anything like this in my life. I'm just not sure how I will handle knowing that I fathered a child. You will be all right I know you will, I said. It wasn't long before we arrived. Amanda met us at the door and let us in. I see you brought the little one with you. Yes we decided to bring her along, Harry said. Amanda this is my fiance' Maria Dolace. Nice to meet you Maria.

It's a pleasure to meet you too Amanda. Dr.
Michaels is expecting you. Go right in. Hello
Dr. Michaels how are you? Good Harry. Dr. this
Maria, my fiance' and this is Kaitee. Hello
Maria, pleasure to meet you both. Thank you Dr.
Michaels. Have a seat he said as he closed the
door. I assume everyone is knowledgeable about
why we are here today? Yes, Dr. we don't have
any secrests. Good to hear, he said. He sat
down to his desk and opened the file. Harry you
are the father of this little girl. There is no
doubt about it she is your daughter. Harry
hands covered his face. He couldn't decide
whether he was happy or sad at that moment. I
placed my hand on his back. You all right
Harry? He pulled his hands away. Yes, I think
I am. Now I don't have to fight to keep her, he
said. Dr. Michaels, do you have a copy of the

results for me? Yes this is your copy. He handed Harry an envelope. Thank you Dr. Michaels he said as he shook his hand. They said their good byes and left the office. Once in the car, I watched him as he tried not to show emotions. I needed him to be real about what he was feeling but I didn't want to push him. I waited until we were home and Kaitee had finished her bottle. He was standing in the door looking out side. I had Kaitee on my shoulder as I walked over to him. Harry. He was thinking so hard that he didn't hear me calling him. Harry, I said again. Yes, he turned quickly answering me. Don't shut me out. I didn't mean to baby. I'm just so in shock. I don't know what to say. I have a daughter, she really is my child. Yes she is and you will be a great father. Come on Maria, I don't know the first thing about raising a kid. I never had a

good relationship with my father. Harry, that's

not even what it's about. What are you talking

about? I walked over to the playpen and put

Kaitee down. I walked back over to Harry. It's

about the love in your heart. You don't need to

have had a father to be a good one. If you can

love a child like you love yourself, you are

almost there. Sure you will make mistakes but

that's what life is all about. Don't you agree,

I asked? He looked into my eyes. How did I get

so lucky, he said? No, Harry. I am the lucky

one. I am so blessed to have you in my life. I

thought I knew what love was. I was so wrong

Harry. You believe that you loved Kentrel,

Maria. It was a different kind of love, but you

did love him. It was different all right, I

added. Filled with lies and minipulation.

Well, now you know the truth and I am going to do all that I can to make sure you know every day of your life what real love is. You are so good to me Harry Stonewell. He kissed me gently. Harry the feelings I had after Malik raped me are still so fresh. I know it's been months, but sometimes I can feel that cold dead feeling that I had afterwards. Harry just listened as she talked. They had taken a seat on the sofa and Maria crossed her feet under her and sat facing him. I know love, Harry. I have always had the love of my parents. My parents love me no matter who I am or what I do in life. They love me Harry. The love a woman feels for a man is so different. I have watched my parents all of my life and they are not saints. They have had their turn with maritial issues. But they never stopped loving each other. They never stopped showing love for each other. I know this might sound crazy to you Harry. I was with Kentrel but I was the loneliest woman I knew. I remember telling him that I wanted someone just for me. I wanted a man who would love me for more than sex. I want to be helded by a man and have him look into my eyes like my father looks into my mothers eyes. I want to know what it feels like to be loved that way Harry. Have you ever felt that way about anyone? I thought I did. But, I don't want to talk about me right now. He reached for me to come sit by him. I moved over to the side of the sofa with him. He wrapped his arms around my waist. Harry put his chin on my shoulder and spoke softly to me. Maria, you do know unconditional love. You have had it all your life. I think that what you are looking for is receptive love. By that I mean, you want to get back what you are giving. Yes, Harry that is exactly what I mean. If I give you all that I have to give and you give me a few moments of your time, I am the one who has been shorted. Well sweetie, I plan on giving you exactly what you are looking for. It is my desire that you know what true love is. As we grow old together, you will know and experience on a daily basis the meaning of true love. Harry, I don't know what you expect from me? I am not sure of so many things. Maria, patience is what is expected from me and from you. I want to know who you are. I want to learn what your likes and dislikes are. I want to experience everything there is to experience about you. So you see, it's not sexual. It is about the person. I expect us to laugh together, cry together, sing together and yes definitely pray together. I want us to be a strong family. I was so into what he was saying. Harry I am feeling like we can be all the things that you are speaking of. I hear a but in there somewhere, he said. But, I know we have a long road ahead of us, that's all I am saying. I know Maria, but we have already shown that we can handle almost anything. I don't see anything that was thrown at us since we met that we have not been able to handle. Have you? You are right Harry, you are so right. Speaking of challenges, I need to call Thompson. I leaned up so that he could get up. Harry pulled out his cell phone and dialed Thompson's number. Hello, this is Harry Stonewell calling for Mr. Thompson. Hold please, the secretary said. Harry, it's good to hear from you Thompson said as he chimed in to the call. I have that information for you. The test show that she is definitely my daughter. I hope that you are happy with that news. It did throw me for a minute or so. But I am all right with it. When can you get started on that paper work for me? It is ready and waiting on a copy of the paternity test, Thompson replied. Great, I will bring it by in the morning if that is good with you. I will be in court, but you can leave it with Ginger. She will have you sign everything that needs signing. Sounds good and thanks for your help, Harry said. What is going on with the other case. I will need Maria to come in and talk with me one day next week, if it is possible. Yes, we can make that happen. Just let me know when Harry said. When you come in to bring the test results, have Ginger set up a date and time. Thanks man you are the greatest.

Not a problem Harry. You take care.. Harry

ended the call and turned to see Maria curled up

on the sofa with her eyes closed. She looked so

peaceful. He pulled the blanket from the back of

the sofa and covered her up. He sat on the

floor and muted the sound on the tv and flipped

from screen to screen.

Days passed quickly as they settled into a

daily routine. They both returned to work and

Kaitee was being kept by Maria's parents. Harry

decided it was time to introduce Kaitee to her

grandmother. It was Saturday morning and they

had just finished cleaning and washing from the

previous week. Harry told Maria about his

decision along with the fact that he wanted his

mother to keep Kaitee during the day. My

parents will be crushed she said. They have

grown use to having her around. Maybe we can
alternate weeks between the two of them, Harry
suggested. Your mother is closer I said. She
is use to your parents, Harry announced. We
will see he said. My mother is pretty involved
with things outside the house and she has a
schedule of her own, whereas your parents have
already adjusted to having her arround. Yes,
this is true I said. By the way, when are we
going to set a wedding date? He caught me off
guard. I really had not thought about it.
Well, can we do it now, Harry suggested? Let me
get a calendar. I went into the bedroom and
returned with a calendar. I stood behind the
sofa and watched Harry play with his daughter.
She is so happy here, Harry. Yes she is
sweetie. Come on, lets set a wedding date. We
sat on the floor and Kaitee lay on her stomach

playing with the items in front of her. Let's
see, Harry said. Is six months too soon? Yes
it is, I wouldn't have enough time to do
anything. So, are we looking at next year, he
said? I think so. I don't want to wait that
long, he anounced. I looked at him. Why, is
there a problem? You might change your mind, he
said. I don't think so honey, you are not
getting off that easy. We both laughed.
Seriously Maria, I don't want to wait. We can
get married next week and it wouldn't be soon
enough for me. Harry why are you in such a
rush? I am just ready for us to be a family.
We are a family Harry. Can't you see that?
Maria, I mean legally. I know we are both
adults and we can do what ever we want, but in
the eyes of God, we are living in sin. We are
not man and wife. I want to be under the same

roof with you legally. I understand what you are saying Harry. So, when do you want to get married? Tomorrow, he said. Harry be serious. I am. We can get married after church tomorrow. Harry, we don't have marriage licsence. Ok, maybe next Sunday, he said. I want a real wedding, with all the trimmings, I said as my face lit up. How long will it take you to put it together, he asked? I don't know. Let me check on a few things and I can give you an idea later this week. I also brought a note pad to write down some notes. I began by making a note to call the church to see what dates were available for next month. I then noted that I needed to find a dress, call Gayle, Joni, Porcha and my cousin Carlan to see if they would all be bridemaids. I then made a note to call my parents, find a place for the reception and

someone to cater. I turned to Harry. You know
this is going to cost some money don't you?
Maria, whatever we need to do, I am sure we can
handle it. We can split up the duties and that
will make things go so much smoother. Let me
get the church squared away and then we can work
from there. I pulled out the phone book and
called the secretary of Starlight Chapel.
Antionette Chimes is a sweet young lady and very
attentive to church business. She was more than
happy to check the schedule for me. The third
Saturday in October is available, will that be
all right for you? Yes that sounds great.
Would you schedule an appointment for us with
Pastor Martin? How about this week, let's say
Thursday evening around 6:30? Hold on a
minuteTony. Harry can you meet with Pastor
Martin on Thursday at 6:30? Yes I'm available.

Tony, we can be there. Good, I will schedule
you in. See you on Thursday she said. Well, we
have a wedding date. October 15th. Would you
like an afternoon or evening wedding Harry.
Evening is better, don't you think so. Yes, I
want candles I said. October 15th at 6:00 pm, I
wrote in my notes. Now I can check that off.
Moving on to the girls. I called Gayle. Gayle
screamed into the phone. You are going to get
married before me, I can't believe this. Yes, I
am, are you angry with me? No way Maria, I am
so happy for you. Good cause I am going to need
a lot of help to get this wedding off the
ground. What is the date? October 15th. You
are crazy girl, that is just a few weeks from
now. I know, so can you help me. I know you
are planning your own wedding. Girl my wedding
is next year. Yours is right now. I am totally

available. When do you want to get started? Now, can you come over? I am on my way. I hung up the phone from talking to Gayle and stopped for a moment. I think I had better call my parents before they hear it from someone else. You are right, make the call. I am going to call my mother, he said. I called my parents and waited for someone to answer the phone. Hello Dolace residence. Hi daddy, how are you? Hello princess, I'm fine and what about you. I am doning great. Where is mama? She is finishing up in the kitchen, you want to talk to her? Yes, I want to talk to both of you actually. Is something wrong honey? No dad, I just have some news. Wait, let me get your mother. Audrey pick up the phone, it's Maria. She picked up the phone in the kitchen. Hello honey, how are you? I am fine mama how are you?

I am fine. Audrey, Maria has something to tell us. What is it honey, Mrs. Dolace asked? Harry and I have set a date. That is wonderful honey. We are getting married next month. Next month, Mrs. Dolace yelled. Why so soon, Maria, she asked? Well, I wanted to plan for next year but Harry felt it would be better that we go ahead and get married sooner. I agreed with him, Maria said. We don't want to continue being under the same roof and not be married. Well, I must say honey, Harry is a wise man. Yes he is daddy. Mama, will you help me with the arrangements? Yes, honey I will help you. Gayle is on her way over, do you want to come over? I will be there shortly. Thanks, I love you both. We love you too honey. They ended their call. Harry was still talking to his mother. He ended his call as well. How did it go with your parents he asked? Fine mama is on her way over and so is Gayle. How about you and your mother? She is excited for us and angry that I have not brought the baby or you by to see her. I tell you what, when your mother and Gayle gets here, I will take Kaitee to see her grandmother. Sounds good, I will get her bag together. The door bell rang and Harry got up to answer the door. It was Gayle. They said their hello's and Gayle congratulated him on setting the date. She had so much stuff with her. She sent Harry to the car to get the rest of the items she brought with her. She held Kaitee until he returned. She was sitting to the table when I came from the bedroom. Hey you, Gayle said when she saw me come out. Hey, Isaid back. They hugged each other. Kaitee gurgled as they talked over her noise. I

brought the invitation book with me, Gayle said.
I think we will have to do them on the computer
since the date is so close, I said. You are soo
right. We can write it up, then go pick up the
paper. Harry walked in with the items. Where
do you want me to put all of this? Put them
right here Gayle said as I cleared the table.
Harry, I will need an address list from you.
Will you ladies permit me to take care of the
reception? Do you want to do this by your self
Harry, Gayle asked. It would be my pleasure.
You all will have your hands full with getting
dresses and decorating the church. Let me
handle the reception. Ok, Harry you got it.
Kaitee and I will go into the bedroom and make
some plans. They all laughted. He went into
the room and called the man that he purchased
the ring from. He made arrangements for a band

to compliment the engagement ring he had given her and for a band for himself. He also got the number from him for his friend Earl Caughgan. Earl is well known for catering large upscale weddings and dinner parties. He dialed his private number. Earl speaking. Earl this Dr. Harry Stonewell. Hello Doctor, what can I do for you. I was told that you can make the impossible happen. Yes I can, he said. Who recommended you? Mr. Chandler. Wonderful he said. Only a select few have my private number. If he gave it to you, you must be very special indeed. I would think so, Harry said. What can I do for you Dr. Stonewell? I need a miracle on October 15th. I see. I am planning my wedding reception and I need the works. For how many guest. About two hundred. Do you have a place? No, I don't. All right so you need a place to hold two hundred people. Let me get all the information from you and I will see what I can do for you. Harry hung up the phone and changed Kaitee's diaper. By the time he finished his cell phone was ringing. Dr. Stonewell, this is Earl. I have a place for you and I can accommodate you on the October 15th. Where is the place, Harry asked? The Breau View Hall on Main Street. That's great, Harry said. Dr. Stonewell how long is the wedding ceremony? It shouldn't take more than an hour. All right, since you don't know what colors, we will do the neutral scene. I will use ivory and gold with greenery. Hold on Earl. Maria he yelled outside the door. What are the colors? Ivory and burgundy, she said. Ivory and burgundy he relayed to Earl. Wonderful, when can I expect you to sign my contract? Special messenger it to me at the hospital and I will send the check back with the contract. Wonderful doing business with you Dr. Stonewell. Same here Earl. Harry walked out of the room with Kaitee. My job is done, he announced. What, Gayle said. I am done. I have the reception taken care of. How could you have done that in so little time, Maria asked? One name, he said. "Earl Caughgan". Now way! No way, Harry, Gayle said. I have been trying to contact this man for six months and you get him in one day. No way. Yes way and he even found a place for the reception. Where, Maria asked? Breau View Hall. Wait aminute, that place has been booked since last year, Gayle announced. Well, I don't know how he got it, I just know that he has. If you need me to call him for you Gayle I will? Yes, I would like that very much Harry, Gayle said.

How are the plans coming for the dresses? We
are getting there Maria said. All right, if
you don't need me Kaitee and I are going to see
her grandmother. He kissed Maria on the lips
and then let her kiss Kaitee and they were off.
That man really loves you Maria. I know she
said as her lips curled up into a smile. Why
don't we go to the bridal shop and try on some
dresses? Sure, mama will be here in a few
minutes and then we can all leave. They wrote
up what was to be printed on the wedding
invitations and chose the color paper. They
heard Mrs. Dolace pull up and met her at the
door. Hi mama, we are going to look at wedding
dresses hop into Gayle's car. I thought we were
just making plans. Mama, we don't have a lot of
time so we will try to find some dresses as soon

as possible. Ok, honey whatever you want to do
is fine with me.

CHAPTER TWENTY

They pulled up to a shop called "You are the bride". They went in and began looking around. It was evident that Gayle and Mrs. Dolace had different ideas of my style of dress. Gayle pulled out something that was too revealing and Mrs. Dolace showed me a dress that went all the way up to my neck. I shook my head no to both dresses. I walked around to another isle and began looking at the dresses on the rack. I had something in mind and had not seen anything that came close to it. Finally, a woman walked up to assist me. I explained what I had in mind and the woman asked me to join her in a room in the back. Gayle and Mrs. Dolace followed us into the room. The woman introduced herself as Melanie and Maria introduced herself along with Gayle and Mrs. Dolace. Melanie asked me to join

her behind a wall and try on a dress she had
hanging up. I saw the dress and thought I would
faint. It was perfect.   It was everything I
had imagined.   I put the dress on and walked
out to show my mother and Gayle. Oh my God,
Gayle said as she gazed at her best friend.
Mrs. Dolace covered her mouth as tears fell from
her eyes. You are beautiful Gayle said.   I
don't believe this, Gayle said. This is the
dress you have been talking about this morning.
Yes it is, I said. The dress was Ivory taffita
with extra wide shoulder straps that gathered at
the top. There were the most beautiful closed
roses that set on the top of the shoulder
straps. The bodice was designed with pearls
that trimmed the v-shaped neck line. The
material the made up the bodice was brocade
ivory with a hint of mauve. The pearlesque

pearls accented the colors magnicifently. On the back of the dress the zipper is covered with tiny off white roses the come down to the bottom of the bodice, which is also trimmed with the pearls. Three medium size roses center a large ivory bow which flows on top of the medium length train. The train was also decorated with pearls. This dress was made for Maria. Within an hour I had found the perfect dress. What about the head piece, Mrs. Dolace asked? Melanie went around the wall and returned with another piece that complimented the dress. This is it, I said. The complete package. Simple and elegant I whispered. The band of pearls that flowed across my forehead were about an inch and a half in diameter and the pearls matched the pearls on the dress perfectly. I don't need to look any further, I said. This is it. Melanie did a few pins for alterations to the sides and the hem line. I took off the dress and veil. Now all we need to do is find dresses for the rest of you, I said. Melanie, can we see bridemaids dresses and something for my mother? Sure, let's move to another room. They walked across the hall into another room. How many dresses will you need? Four bridemaids and one dress for my mother and something for my mother in law to be. What are your colors? I want my maids in burgundy and the maid of honor in ivory. I want my mom in ivory and his mother in burgundy. All right, lets see what we can fine. Melanie had a few of the other girls that worked in the store bring in some dresses for Gayle and I to look at. Gayle liked one in particular and it almost resembled the style of my wedding gown. What about this one in Ivory?

Melanie pulled a few dresses apart on the rack and pulled the ivory dress out. What size do you need? I think I will need a 12 or 13 Gayle said. I believe we can alter this for you. Now what about the other ladies? There are three others and I will send them over as soon as possible. What about my mother, I asked. Come with me Mrs., I'm sorry what is your name? Dolace, Audrey Dolace. Mrs. Dolace, lets take a look at what we have for you. What size do you wear? They went on down the hall and out of ear range. One of the other sales ladies began to measure Gayle for the dress. What do you think Maria, Gayle asked? I think you are lovly in it. Gayle detected something in Maria's voice. After she and the sales lady finished she dressed and sat beside me. What's up girl? This is all so overwhelming Gayle. I don't know if I can do this. You are doing it Maria. You and Harry will be fine. You know that don't you? Yes, I do but I would like more time to do it. I can understand that girl. I am glad I have the time to plan my wedding. With all I have going on, I need the time to get things done. What do you need me to do, Gayle asked? I don't know right now. Just then Mrs. Dolace entered the room with a beautiful dress. I love it mama. Yes, Mrs. Dolace it is beautiful. Do you need to have it altered? No, it fit perfectly. I just need to have the shoes dyed and that is all. What color tuxedo will your father need honey? Ivory mama. I will have Harry pick daddy up and they will go together. Ms. Dolace how will you be paying for your dress, Michelle asked? Your father and I will pay for your dress, Mrs. Dolace said. Mama, I can't let you guys do that. Maria your father and I have been saving for this day all of our lives. And we are prepared to do this honey and we really want to. I tell you what, why don't we both pay for the dress and you can help me with everything else. All right honey, that sounds like a good idea. So they both wrote out checks to Michelle and Mrs. Dolace paid seperately for her dress. What about Angel honey is she going to be in the wedding? Oh yes she can be my miniature bride or the flower girl. I will bring her back one day doing the week to get her fitted for a dress, Maria told her mother. They finished up at the bridal shop and headed home. Once they made it to Maria's home, Mrs. Dolace did not come in side. She gave both girls a hug and went home. Maria and Gayle finished up their planning and Maria made

the other calls she needed to make. Gayle was
having dinner with her fiance' so she had to
leave. Harry phoned to say that he and Kaitee
were on their way home. I locked up after Gayle
left and began fixing dinner. I had a chill run
over her body and it spooked me. I felt like
someone was watching me. I became nervous and
felt like I couldn't breath. I thought of Harry
and began to calm down a bit. I decided to do
something I had not done in a long time. I took
a seat at the kitchen table and began to pray.
I could feel the tenseness leave my body. I
recalled one of the conversations I had with
Helen, my therapist. I prayed for the strength
to release the feelings I had towards Malik. I
knew that as long as I held hatred for him in my
heart, I would never be free. Is it the fear of
him that is holding me down? God remove it from

me. Forgiveness is what you are showing me but, how can I forgive him Lord? How do I show kindess for someone who would hurt me this way? Tears began to fall from her eyes. I don't understand why I have to forgive him? God help me to understand. I dried my face and stared into space for a little while. I took a deep breath, walked over to the cabinet got a clean glass and poured some ice tea. I felt a calmness now instead of the fear that had gripped me earlier. The door bell rang and I walked over to the door. Oh God why are you testing me like this. I looked again to be sure that the person standing on the other side was actually who I saw the first time. I opened the door. Kentrel what are you doing here? I know you told me to go away Maria, but I just needed to see you. May I come in? Why, do you want to rape me too? Maria I would never hurt you. I really need to talk to you, it's really important. Maria please. Come in Kentrel. He walked past her and into the living room. No, I want you to sit here at the table. Kentrel did as she asked. He walked up to her first. I am so sorry that Malik hurt you. He reached out his hand to touch her face and she quickly moved away from him. Don't touch me, I just can't handle that. I'm sorry Maria. I thought.. What did you think Kentrel? That you could just come back here and every thing would be the way it was? I will never be the same again. It is hard for me to let my father hug me, and you think I would allow you to touch me? What do you want Kentrel? Maria sit down. I sat at the table on the opposite side from him. I have something to tell you. What is it? Malik won't

be bothering you ever again. I know that
Kentrel he is in jail. No, Maria, he's dead.
What? Malik is dead, Maria. It happened at the
prison. There was a fight and he was involved.
Someone stabed him. I stood up and walked away
from the table. I don't know what to say. I
don't even know what to feel. I turned and
walked over to Kentrel. Did you do this? He
wouldn't look at me. I can't answer that Maria.
Kentrel did you have anything to do with this?
I just wanted you to know, so you wouldn't be
afraid any more. I covered my mouth with both
hands. Kentrel was standing now and facing me.
He was looking at my hands. He looked away. I
realized that he had seen the ring on my finger.
So, are you happy with him Maria? I looked at
my hand with the ring on it and back at Kentrel.
Yes, I'm happy Kentrel. Harry makes me very

happy. Matter of fact we are getting married next month. It was a large pill for him to swallow, but he did. Congratulations Maria, you deserve to be happy. Now you have someone just for you. Thank you Kentrel. She walked him to the door and just as she opened it, Harry and Kaitee were standing there about to come in. Is everything all right, Harry asked. Yes, it is Harry. Harry this is Kentrel, Kentrel this is my fiance' Harry and our daughter Kaitee. Kentrel held out his hand to Harry. Harry paused and then shook his hand. I reached for Kaitee and turned to Harry. Kentrel was delivering news about Malik. Is that right, Harry said with sarcasm. Yes, it seems that he was killed in a prison fight. I wanted Maria to know that she didn't have to be afraid anymore. It seems the least I could do, Kentrel said.

Harry didn't respond. Well, I need to be going now, oh congratulations. I hope the two of you will be very happy. Thank you Kentrel and thanks for letting me know what happened. Harry was still standing with his arms folded across his chest with the cast hand on top. I closed the door behind him and turn to face Harry. We were both silent for a moment. He scooped Kaitee out of my arms and put her in the play pen. Maria, why did you let him in? Kentrel is not a threat to me Harry. You didn't think Malik was either when you let him in. I put my right hand on my forehead and took a deep breath. Harry, Kentrel would never hurt me, I know him. You are too tursting Maria. Harry he just wanted me to know so that I wouldn't be afraid any more. He didn't respond to me. You don't have to worry about Kentrel, Harry. He knows that we are getting married. You also knew that he was married and you continued to see him Maria. You want to tell me that you don't think he is a threat? I couldn't take it anymore. I stormed out of the living room into the bedroom and slammed the door. Harry paced the floor as Kaitee watched him. That woman, that woman, he said with clenched teeth. He stopped pacing and went into the kitchen to warm the baby food. He picked Kaitee up, placed her in the highchair and began feeding her. I guess I will give her some time to calm down he whisphered to Kaitee. I fell across the bed crying. I don't know why I was crying. It could be a combination of things. Harry being angry with me, knowing that Kentrel probably had something to do with Malik's death, or even the fact that as much as I had said I wanted him dead, I really didn't mean it. I guess it took me longer to come out than Harry had imagined. Kaitee was asleep in the play pen. It must have been over a half an hour later when Harry came into the room. I was still sniffling when he walked in. He walked around the bed so that he could face me and sat down. I'm sorry I yelled at you. He brushed the hair away from my face. Baby, come on talk to me, he said. He got a tissue from the tissue box on the night stand and dabbed away the tears from my face. Would you sit up and talk to me please? I took a deep breath and sat up in the bed. Baby, I know that I need to trust your judgment. You trust Kentrel and I don't. I handled the situation wrong and I am sorry. That doesn't mean that I want to see him in our home. He is apart of your past Maria and I think he should stay

there. So you get to make all the rules Harry?
No, that is not what I am saying. So, Harry,
Kaitee is your past should we leave her in the
past too? She is a product of you and Gina,
Harry. Is that not the past? Harry stood up
and walked away for the bed as he spook. Woman,
don't you understand that I am jealouse of your
past with him? He got to hold you and make love
to you and every time I see him it reminds me of
that fact.   I hung my feet over the side of the
bed and looked up at him. I'm sorry that my
past hurts you so much. We can make new
memories Harry. Your thoughts of me and Kentrel
will no longer exist. Harry moved closer to me
and lifted me from the bed. Do you know how
much I want to make love to you? I am a patient
man but sometimes it's just hard to fight the
flesh. I don't know what will happen if and

when we do make love Harry. I know that I want you, but I just don't know. I don't want this to ruin our wedding night Harry. I have so many emotions bottled up inside and I don't know what to do. Shhh, I am pushing you into something that you are not ready for, Maria. Look we are exchanging our vows before God, our family and friends. This is not about us making love. When we make love, it will be right for the both of us. I have faith in myself that I can handle waiting until you are ready. I want you to have faith in your self, and when that time comes, you will let me know. Now lets see what we have left of our wedding plans, and you can tell me about this dress, I've been hearing about. Harry you have been listening to our conversations. Well when you women get started, you don't pay attention to who is in the room with you. They walked into the kitchen and sat to the table. I pulled out my notes and we finalized what was left of the plans. I have a surprise for you during the ceremony so when you have them printed, leave a space after the prayer. What are you up to Harry? Just put in the space "Groom". Harry! Just do it Maria. You will have to wait and see. I made the notes on about what Harry wanted. Harry where are you going to get your tuxedo? I will out check a few places tomorrow. What color am I wearing? Ivory. What about the groomsmen? Everyone of you will be in Ivory. The groomsmen will have burgundy cummerbunds, and yours and daddy's will be ivory. I have ordered the boutineieres and flowers. Oh yeah, sweetie I have taken care of the rings. I crossed that off the list as well. Do you have someone to play the music Maria?

Yes, I have it covered. Are we forgetting anything, he asked? Just as he finished the question, Kaitee began to cry. Oh yeah, we don't have anything for Kaitee to wear. I trust that you will handle that, he said? Yes, I will handle it. I have to take Angel to get fitted for her dress and I will find something for Kaitee. Come here woman so I can hug you. I got up and sat on Harry's lap. You are wonderful. I knew you could get this wedding off the ground. I hope it goes just like we are planning it, Harry. Everything will be fine sweetie, just fine.

CHAPTER TWENTY-ONE

Weeks past and the wedding day was fast approaching. I was a nervous reck. I had everything in order. However, I was waiting for the bomb to drop. Usually, something always went wrong when there was a big event. The girls at the office gave me a bridal shower after work in the conference room. Harry was in on it. I was upset because Milton called a manditory after hours staff meeting. I thought he had lost his mind. I needed to pick up Kaitee and handle a few things for the wedding. I called Harry to pick up Kaitee. I mumbled under my breath as I headed down the hall for the conference room. I opened the door and they all yelled "Surprise". I almost fell backwards. I could not believe that they had planned this right under my nose. I guess I was so busy, I had not notice anything going on in the office. We all laughed as they told me how several people in the office almost spoiled the surprise. Gayle admitted that she had the worst time keeping the secret because she was always with me. I am so glad this day is here and over, cause I don't think I could get around Maria one more day Gayle said with laughter. We all laughed at her. Several of my co-workers made toast and gave their advice for a long and loving marriage. Gayle stood up and quieted everyone so that she could speak. Maria, you are my dearest and best friend since our school days. I have loved you as my friend and sister. I bless the day Harry came into your life. I believe God made the two of you and destined you to meet. To a precious marriage for two very precious people. Congratulations. Everyone

raised their glasses in agreement to Gayles

toast. It's time for gifts, Gayle announced.

We spent the next half hour opening gifts,

laughing and teasing. We had light refreshments

and Gayle asked me to say a few words. I stood

up and looked around the room. I don't know how

to express to you all how you make me feel. I

was surprised beyond degree when I opened that

door. Milton, I thought you had just lost your

mind about a manditory meeting. Everyone

laughed. Seriously, guys I couldn't find a

better place to work and better friends to work

with. I am so appreciative of all you have done

to make me feel safe and loved in this place. I

love each and everyone of you. Everyone gave

her a hug and they began to clean up the

conference room. It was forty-five minutes past

the quiting time. Everyone was rushing to get their things together to leave for the day. Harry walked through the door looking like a million bucks. Hello sweetness. I turned at the sound of his voice. What are you doing here? I came to help you bring your gifs to the car. Gayle came back to the room with a cart to push the gifts on. They loaded the gift bags and boxes onto the cart and Harry took them to the car. He returned to walk her out. Milton this my fiance' Harry Stonewell. Harry this is our CEO, Milton Dawson. It's a pleasure to meet you Milton. The pleasure is all mine Harry. You have found a wonderful person in Ms. Dolace. I know Milton. Look you guys go ahead and I will lock up the office, Milton said. We will see you tomorrow, Maria. Thanks again guys. Harry wrapped his arm around my waiste and we headed out of the conference room. I need to stop by my office to get my purse. I opened the door and we walked inside. Harry closed the door behind him. Why did you close the door, we're not staying. I picked up my purse and walked towards him. So this is your office. Yes, this is my office. What is up with you Harry? He pulled me close to him, I don't know, he whispered and kissed me on the lips. Everything is coming together for us and it feels so right, so good. Do you feel it baby? I smiled at him. Yes baby, I feel it too. With his arms holding me close and his lips on mine, I felt like someone I use to know. I felt like a woman in love and it felt so good. As he removed his lips from mine, I said something to him that I had not said before. I love you Harry. I will never forget the look in his

eyes. He almost cried. He hugged me so tight.
Oh baby, I love you too, he said. Gayle knocked
on the door. You guys going home tonight or are
we locking you in? She realized she had bad
timing. Is everything all right? Maria just
grabbed her and hugged her too. Yes, Gayle
everything is better than all right. Harry
turned away as he wiped the moisture from his
eyes. Gayle had a strange look on her face. I
mouthed to her that "I told him I loved him".
She took a deep breath and hugged me again. She
pulled away and mouthed back, "I'm so happy for
you". What are you two doing, Harry asked?
Just girl talk, I said. I didn't hear any
words, he said. You would have to be a girl to
understand Harry, I told him. He shook his
head. Let's go home, he said. See you later
Gayle, we both said. The evening was smooth

and uneventful. They both worked on their separate agendas and finally went to bed.

Harry went into his office bright and early the next day. He was looking over a file when his cell phone began to ring. He did not recognize the number but he answered it. Hi Harry, it's me Gina. Harry held the phone without saying a word. Harry are you there? Yes I'm here. I know you probably don't want to talk to me. Yes, Gina you would be right, I don't. How is Kaitee? Kaitee is doing fine. She has everything she needs. I hope you understand that I did what I did out of love for her. Your intentions may have been good towards Kaitee, Gina but you were mostly looking our for yourself. Harry that's not true. Gina what do you want? I want to see how you were doing with our daughter. Well, we are doing just fine with

out you in our lives. Harry wait! I realize
that I am messed up and all I want is to be able
to see her sometimes. Gina where are you? I
can't tell you that Harry. Good bye Gina. He
pressed the button on the phone disconnecting
the call. I am sick and tired of your games
Ginerette. This is the last one you will ever
get away with. He dialed Thompson's office and
told him that he had just had contact with
Ginarette and that she would not give him her
where-abouts. He gave Thompson the phone number
that she called from to check it out. I want to
proceed with custody of my daughter right away.
After Maria and I are married we will need the
adoption paper-work drawn up for Maria to become
her mother legally. I will get right on it
Harry. They ended their call and Harry sat back
in his chair. I want you out of our lives Gina,

he said out loud. Thompson called the number
that Harry had given him. The phone rang
continueously. He call the operator and had the
number checked out. Of course it was a pay
phone. He was certain that Gina did not want to
be found. He could proceed with Harry's case of
abandoment.

Harry placed another call. This time it was
to his mother. He wanted to see if she had
everything she needed for their wedding. Son, I
am so proud of you. I never liked that girl you
brought here before. I know Maria will make a
fine wife for you and a good mother for my
grand-daughter. Thanks mom, I am the happiest
man alive. I have slacked on one issue but we
can handle this after the wedding. What is it
Harry? A house, I need a house for my family.
Both of our apartments are small. I know Maria

would be more than happy to move out of her apartment. Would you mind talking to your friend who does realestate? No problem son. I'll have Janet give you a call. I love you mama, talk to you later. I think I have everything in place now, he said to himself.

CHAPTER TWENTY-TWO

Over at my office I was sitting at my desk
putting together the ceremony to have it
printed. I decided on a bouquet of roses with
doves holding the ribbon ends that are tied
around the flowers. I chose cream paper with
black print. Once I finished writing everything
out, I typed it. I had Gayle proof it.
Everything looks fine to me she said. But why
do you have "Groom" written here? Well, Harry
has a surprise and this is what he asked me to
put in this space. Ok, Gayle said. I am too
curious about this surprise. Harry is full of
surprises Gayle, you will learn that about his
as you get to know him. You talk as if you have
known him for years. It sure feels that way,
Gayle. I need to drop this off at the printers.

Would you like to go with me? Yes, sure. Maybe we can grab lunch while we are out. Sounds good to me.

The weeks before the wedding turned into days and Maria spent most of her days handling last minute wedding business. It was Sunday morning and they were getting ready for church. I finshed dressing Kaitee and went to the mirror to finsih putting on her makeup. Harry came in and picked Kaitee up. Hello precious, are you ready for church? Kaitee laughed as he lifted her in the air and back down to his face. I quietly watched from the mirror as I applied lipstick to my lips. I fluffed my hair and lightly sprayed perfume. You guys ready I called out? Ready when you are he said. Look at my two girls, Harry said. You two are beautiful. You're not so bad yourself, I replied. Are we going to your parents afterwards to eat dinner, he asked? Yes that is the plan. Do you want to do something different? No that's fine. I just wanted to know. Maria's suit was brown and tan with designs and the pumps and purse matched. Kaitee's dress was tan and burgundy and lace around the bottom. She had the cutiest little bow. Kaitee's hazel brown eyes and caramel brown skin seemed to be a blend of Maria and Harry. If you didn't know it you would think that she was theirs together. Are we bringing the seat into the church he asked. Maybe we should, just in case she goes to sleep. You have your bible, he asked? Yes it's right here. All right, we are ready. Harry got the car seat and headed for the car. I had the baby and we were on their way. Starlight Chapel was about a twenty minute ride for them. They arrived and I was waiting for Harry to get the baby out of the car. It had been a while since I had been to church and I was a little squemish about my return. There was one person I really did not want to encounter. Adrenna. Harry could sense my nervousness. Are you all right? I 'm fine, I replied. He brushed the hair from my eyes and asked me again. Are you really all right? I smiled at him. I will be fine. He rubbed his hand over my back. It's all right sweetie. Kaitee was squirming in her seat. He stopped and took her out while Maria picked up the carrier. Oh, I forgot my bible, I said. Well, here you take her and I will go back to the car. Church had not started yet, so I was able to go right in and find a seat. Kaitee was wide awake and ready to play. She grabbed at my hair as we

walked in. I could feel eyes on me as I walked
in. I decided not to pay attention to them. I
took a seat and sat Kaitee on my lap. Harry
returned and sat beside me placing the carrier
on the floor under the pew in front of us. Mrs.
Sara came in and headed right over to us. I
stood up and we hugged each other so tightly
while Harry held Kaitee. It is so good to see
you Maria, she said. It is good to see you too
Mrs. Sara. Good morning mama Harry said. Good
morning son and how is my little pudding cup?
Kaitee giggled at her while chewing on her
fingers. I reached over and dried her mouth and
hands with the diaper cloth. Mrs. Sara sat on
the other side of Harry. She normally sits up
front but I guess she wanted to be with us
today. As I looked around the church, I could
only imagine what was going through some of the

peoples minds. Especially because of the looks and whispers. They are probably thinking that this is my baby. Maybe they are thinking that this is why I had not been to church in a long time. Harry caught the look on my face and brushed his hand over my cheek. Hey you. I smiled a little. He leaned over and whispered into my ear. Relax, you are in good hands. Mine and Gods. I couldn't help but feel a sense of releif after hearing that. I saw mama and Angel come in and Angel waved at me. Mama took her usual seat up front. Angel would not sit still and mama finally allowed her to come to me. Hello angel face, I said to her. Hi sister, I love you. I don't know why she said it like that but I responded to her with I love you too. She sat quietly as she held Kaitee's hand. The music began to play and the choir marched in. We all stood up and sang along with the choir.

The message was good, and good for the soul. Pastor spoke about christain responsibility. The message hit home as usual. I took it all in and wrote down a few scriptures for meditation. As Antoinette read the announcements, she came to our wedding invitation. She read it and of course everyone turned and looked our way. Harry felt proud, and I felt nervous. I moved my attention to Kaitee who was about to cry. She was hungry. I asked Harry for the small bottle from the bag. I gave her the bottle and held onto it along with her holding it too. Pastor gave the benediction and church was over. Pastor always walked out first and greeted everyone that came. We waited around in our seats for mama to come by. Hi mama, how are you? I am good now that I can see you here again. I smiled faintly. I hate it when she is so blunt. I know she disapproves of us sleeping under the same roof. I could see the disappointment in her eyes everytime we go over to pick up Kaitee. I hope after the wedding she will be over it. Sometimes I feel as if I have strained our relationship. Maybe we need to spend some time together. But I knew that the wedding was next weekend. What time did I have to spare? Kaitee saw her and began reaching for her. Come here sugar, she said. Look how pretty you are today. Good morning Harry, she said. Good morning Mrs. Dolace he said as he leaned over and kissed her on the cheek. I hope you cooked plenty for dinner, cause I am starving. It's good to have someone come over with a healthy appetite like yours son. Thanks mom, he said. I will see you all at the house. Mama is something wrong, I asked? I'm just feeling a little tired lately. Ok, we will see you at the house. Mrs. Dolace and Angel walked out of the church.

What I did not know was that Adrenna had been making statements around the church about the rape. She told some of the members that her cousin was killed because of me. She said that I was seeing Kentrel and Malik at the same time. Another lie was that when Kentrel found out that I was sneaking around with Malik that's when I said that Malik raped me. My mama heard all the lies and was sick and tired of having to fight them off. Mrs. Sara told these things to Harry and Harry of course had already confided in her that he was the one who found me after the rape had just taken place. So, she did not believe the lies that were being spreaded. My mama was so tired of hearing things about me that it worried her. I gave the baby to Harry and asked Pastor Martin if he could talk with me for a few minutes. I asked him if he would speak to my mother and help her to see that lies are always going to be told. Especially when people don't know the truth they create their own version and spread it like the truth. Pastor commended me on my view in light of all that has happened to me. He said that he would definitely speak with my mother. He also asked if I would mind if he had a few words with the congregation on gossip. I told him that I would not mind at all. I brought him over to introduce him to Kaitee. He held her for a brief moment. She was so into her bottle that she didn't have time to play with Pastor Martin. We were finally ready to leave the church, when Adrenna came from out of no where. Well, well, well, I see you decided to come out of hiding. Harry stepped in between the two of us. It's ok Harry. Let her say what ever she has to say. I just want to tell you that you are a dispicable little whore and that you got just what you deserved. That is enough, Harry said as he slid between them again. How could you speak like that in the house of the Lord, Harry asked? Pastor Martin overheard every word Adrenna said. He walked up behind her. Adrenna come with me please. They walked up towards the pulpit. We could hear him letting her have it. I overheard him telling her to do what was right or else. She walked towards me. Maria, I know that you did not kill my cousin and I am sorry for what I said. I don't know why you would say that he raped you?

Harry had Kaitee on his chest. He moved closer to Adrenna. She said he did because he almost knocked me down when he was leaving her apartment. I was the one who found her after he raped her. I was the one standing at the door when he opened it and ran out. Is that enough reason, for you. Harry, you don't owe anyone an explanation. It's over and that's the way it should stay. Adrenna, had a look of shame on her face. Harry whispered to her. If you would put more time into finding out the truth in stead of being angry about something that you don't know anything about, you would be a better person than you are. Maria didn't ask to be raped Adrenna. No woman ask to be hurt that way. You are a woman, think about that the next time you decide to talk about another woman. Let's go Maria. He was angry. Pastor Martin you have a good day, he said to him. Thank you son. There were people standing around to see what was going to happen between me and Adrenna. Evidently she had given the impression that she was going to hurt me. Some how I don't think it happened the way she intended. Harry and I walked past everyone and out to the parking lot. He strapped Kaitee into her seat and walked around the car to open the door for me. He turned me around to him. Don't you ever let anyone think that they have the right to say just anything to you. Harry I don't owe anyone an explanation about what happened. Let them think what they want. I know the truth and that's all that matters. He held my face with his hands and kissed me gently on the lips. I'm sorry I got so angry back there. You were standing up for me. It's what men do. I

understand. Let's go home baby he said. He
closed the door behind me and went around to get
in. There were still people standing out side
the church watching. He shook his head.
Everyone wants to attend a show don't they? Yes
Harry, unfortunately they do.

CHAPTER TWENTY-THREE

Dinner at my parents was all right. We ate and Angel made a fuss over Kaitee, while mama fussed to keep Angel away from Kaitee. Harry and I cleaned up the dishes and talked quietly. Mama, finally sat down and put her feet up. Once we finished the dishes, I joined mama and daddy in the den. I took off my heals and took a seat on the sofa. Harry went into my old bedroom to change Kaitee's diaper. I was so tired that I had fallen asleep on the sofa. They let me sleep for a little while.

I opened my eyes while listening to Harry tell my parents about what happened at church. Your daughter has some spunk he said. I really do believe she is going to be all right. Right now she is more worried about you all than she

is about her self. I knew she was strong but…
Mr. Dolace looked up and realized that she was
awake. He nodded his head in my direction. I
see sleeping beauty is awake, Harry said as he
bounced Kaitee on his knee. Did you feed her
Harry? Yes, I feed her. Well you'd better stop
bouncing her before you are cleaning it up off
the floor. Where is mama and Angel? They are
out back. I got up and stretched for a moment.
I took Kaitee, cleaned her face, then walked out
back with mama and Angel. Angel was playing in
her kitchen while mama read a book. When I
walked through the door with Kaitee, mama put
the book down and reached for the baby. I sat
in a chair across from her. We were both quiet.
Mama, what's wrong? What makes you think
anything is wrong? Mama, your silence is always
the result of something that you think you

shouldn't say. You can say anything you want

mama. I just need you to talk to me. Maria you

are moving too fast. I wish you would think

about this. Mama, how do you feel about Harry?

Maria this has nothing to do with how I feel

about Harry. This is about you. I need to know

something honey. Are you marring Harry because

you love him? It is strange you should ask that

question mama. A little while ago I asked

myself that same question. It was just recently

that I realized the answer to that question.

Mama, I finally know what true love is all

about. It's everything I have been taught my

entire life. I never really thought about it

before. My feelings for Harry have been tested

over and over again. I even tried to tell

myself that I would come to love him like he

loves me. I cared for him because he helped me

through a horrible ordeal in my life. Maria

that's what I'm talking about. You are not in

love with this man. Mama, you are so wrong.

Mama I had to disect my feelings into little

bitty pieces. There was a point when I told him

that I could not marry him because I was not

sure of what I felt for him. He gave me time to

figure out what I wanted and what I was feeling.

I am not being pressured into marriage, mama. I

have fallen in love with Harry and mama, for the

first time in my life, I understand what that

means. Those are the conditions that I accepted

Harry's proposal. Not the one that meant I just

needed someone in my life. What I am feeling

for Harry is real and I want to experience real

love. I want to love and be loved the way you

and daddy love each other as man and wife. I

worry about you so much Maria. Mama, it's your

job to worry about me. But, guess what? I am going to be fine. So much has happened Maria. I just want you to be happy. I am happy Mama. They both stood up and hugged each other with Kaitee between them. I think it's time for us to head home. I walked over to escort Angel inside and mama brought Kaitee in. We said our goodbyes and were off to my apartment.

The ride home was quiet. You and your mother have a good talk. Yes we did. You wanna talk about it? She was just worried about me and wondered if I was doing the right thing. I see, he said. Harry, it has nothing to do with you. She loves you. It's me and everything that have taken place in my life. I assured her that I have it under control. Monday morning came and I had work up to my eye balls. I needed to finish up a few cases before I would

be off for two weeks for the wedding. I needed
to be finished with everything by Wednesday
afternoon. Milton had given me two days off
before the wedding. There was one case that was
giving me the blues. I could not satisfy this
client no matter what I gave him. I had to do a
little more research with limited time on my
hands. After about two hours of slaving over a
few books and going through a few files, I found
the answer to our problem. I compiled a new
report and emailed it to Milton for his opinion
and began wrapping up a few other incomplete
assignments. The week began to slow down as
Wednesday rolled around. The client accepted
the last proposal and that made my day.

I was so tired and needed to relax.
Wednesday morning Harry saw the stress on my
face and he knew that I needed a diversion. He

called his mother and arranged for her to baby sit Kaitee. He picked up some flowers for me and went to his apartment to shower and dress. He picked up Kaitee from Mrs. Dolace and dropped her off at his mothers house. It was about 4:30 in the evening and he knew that I would be packing up to head home. He rushed back to my apartment so that he would be there waiting for me. It took me about fifteen minutes to make it from the down town area. I was ready for a long soak in the tub and putting my feet up. I pulled up beside Harry's truck. What is he doing here so early, I said to myself? Harry stepped out of the truck with the bouquet of flowers. Hello sweetness. Harry you look so handsome. What's going on? Well, I noticed how tired you were and I decided to do something about it. I am taking you out to dinner. What about the baby? The baby is in good hands.

Where is she? With my mother. Oh, I said. You

look disapointed. I just look forward to seeing

her little face when I come home. You can see

her little adorable face later. Let's take

these flowers inside and you can change your

clothes.

We walked inside. I was in shock at what I

saw as I walked into the living room. The sofa

was moved to the wall and in the middle of the

floor was a table. There were long stem candles

with champagne chilling. Welcome home,

sweetness. I know you are tired and I knew you

wouldn't want to go out. So, I decided to treat

you to a romantic dinner here at home. Harry

you are so wonderful. I wrapped my arms around

his neck and kissed him. As I removed my lips

from his, he couldn't help but be a little

surprised by the forwardness I displayed. Thank
you, I said. You are most certainly welcome.
He walked over to the candles and lit them.
Give me those, he said as he reached for my
purse, breif case and flowers. He took them
into the bed room and returned to put the
flowers in a vase. He returned to me and pulled
out my chair. Have a seat. I took a seat at
the table. Harry opened the wine and poured
some for the both of us. He picked up his glass
and held it up to me. Here's to you baby. You
are the light of my life. I picked up my glass
and touched it to his. We both sipped from our
glasses. Harry turned and picked up the remote
and pressed the button. He thought of
everything. The soft music began to play. It
was smooth Jazz. It was soft and soothing to my
ears. My I have this dance? I placed the glass

on the table and placed my hand in his. I could not belive what was happening. I knew that I had deep feelings for Harry. But, I learned something tonight. I learned how to fall in love. Harry held me in his arms as if I was a delicate flower. We danced and held on to each other through several songs. This is what was missing from my life. I understand now what Harry meant when he said "its not about the sex". It's about affection and emotions and genuine feelings for your mate. I had resisted the erge to caress his body, or to have him caress mine. It feels so natural. Another song came on and he began to sing in my ear. Oh my God. This man stirred up some emotions in me I had not felt since the last time I had sex with Kentrel. My heart was racing like a speeding car. I was lost in his embrace as his vocals had my mind mesmerized. With my head on his chest and my arms around his waist, we moved to the slow seductive music. Everything was so perfect and so right. Then, the mood was broken with the sound of the door bell. Who could that be, I asked?

Harry didn't say a word. He just released me and walked over to the door. He opened it and several gentlemen walked in with covered trays. Harry returned to me and pulled out my chair. Have a seat please. I sat down to the table and the men carring the trays opened the lids and turned them upside down. They balanced the trays on the lids and placed the plate of food in front of me and one in front of Harry. My God Harry you are unbelievable. I aim to please, he said with a smile on his face. The dish not only smelled delicious, it was beautiful to look at. There was grilled chicken breast surrounded by buttered rice and a mixture of steamed vegetables. Once they finished dressing the table and placed the utensils on in front of us, one of the men asked Harry would there be anything else. He told him that every thing looked fine and that he would signal him for dessert. The man nodded his head and walked out of the door. I was in shock. Harry you did all of this for me. I want to make every day of you life amazing Maria. The day that you are not amazed or unstatisfied is the day I never want to know exist. I blushed as he spoke. You have done so much for me and I feel like all I'm doing is taking. Maria all I want from you is for you to let me love you. Now baby eat your food before it gets cold. We had a wonderful night. After we had dessert, Harry and I slow

danced and enjoyed the rest of the evening.

Mrs. Sara kept Kaitee for the night and that

gave Harry and me a chance to really be alone.

I showered first and he followed. When he came

out of the shower I was in the living room

pouring us another glass of champagne. Harry

walked in with his pajama bottoms and no shirt.

Oh my, he said as his eyes stared my way. You

take my breath away. Thank you sir, I replied.

I had one of the gowns on that he had seen in

the bottom drawer. I had been saving this for a

special occasion. I felt now was as good a time

as any. The silk fushia gown flowed over my

body and did not hide a single curve. The neck

line was v-shaped and reveal enough cleavage to

make a mans mouth water. I handed him his drink

and clicked the remote back on to the slow music

that was playing earlier. I walked over to the sofa and took a seat. Harry was mesmerized by the sight before him. He was choked up and finding it hard to get his words out. I patted the sofa and told him to sit here. I could see him take a deep breath as he walked over and sat on the sofa. He still held the vision in his mind of me turning around and walking over to the sofa. Harry's mind was still on the vision of my long wavy hair flowing down my back covering it right above the point that covered my behind. As I moved the night gown showed my shape and defined my butt cheeks. He heard himself take another breath. In his head he could hear himself say "we shouldn't be here like this". But his heart overruled, or was it his flesh. As he sat beside her, he asked the question. Woman what are you trying to do to me? I am not trying to do anything. I just want to be right here with you. I don't know what is going to happen tonight. I want to just play it by ear, is that all right with you I said? He smiled at me and said "yes that is just fine with me". I put my drink on the end table and turned to face the back of the sofa. I laid across him and placed my head on his chest. He wrapped his arms around me. I could hear his heart beating a little faster. He was aroused and I could feel him. I could tell that he was fighting all the urges and I wasn't helping any. In his mind, he was screaming out, woman you are driving me crazy. I was thinking, it's been along time since these feelings were stired up in me. I was scared of what might happen. But I wanted to make love to Harry. There were so many emotions going on at that moment. Before I realized it Harry's mouth found mine. It was passionate then intense. His grip tightened and I found myself pushing him away. I had to catch my breath. I was fighting a fear that creeped up from the pit of my stomach.

As I lay my head on his chest I could feel the tears run down my face. He could feel the dampness on his chest. He understood without words being said. He ran his hands over my back in a soothing manner. It was a comforting stroke and nothing else. He kissed the top of my head and whispered, it's all right baby, it's all right. We just held each other for a long time without saying anything. I could feel his breathing calm down. But I was angry. I was angry because I allowed the fear to come between me and making love to Harry. I allowed the feeling of being gripped tightly ruin our moment. I recalled Dr. Helen's comments to me about this in one of our sessions. I explained to her that I was afraid. She told me that the only way to get past it was to talk about it. I needed to talk about it with Harry. He needed to know my fears and only then could we work on getting past it. I decided to use her suggestion. Harry? Yes sweetness. I want to talk about what happened. You don't have to explain anything to me baby, I understand that you are not ready. That's not it, Harry. What do you mean? I want to make love to you, I want it so badly but when certain things happen, I just can't. Calm down Maria and breath. I was even having trouble telling him about the feelings I had. I took a deep breathe and let it out. I was fine until you gripped me tightly. I don't know what happened after that. My mind saw him grabbing me and throwing me to the floor. Ok, he said. Maria remember when I told you that the only way to get over something is to face it. Yes, I remember. This is what I meant. I don't know what he did to you. I don't know what happened. You need to get it out in the open between us. I know that it is like reliving it. But baby if you keep it hidden, you will never be able to allow your self to enjoy the pleasures of making love. I would love to touch your body all over. But, I am so afraid of reminding you of something he did to you. I don't know if touching your breast or kissing them will….. At that moment I took his hand and placed it on my breast. I allowed him to caress it. I want to feel you caress my body Harry. I want you to touch me.

I need you to touch me. I kissed his chest and
I could feel his body quiver. His breathing
became rapid. Baby are you sure you want to do
this? I need to do this. I stood up and raised
the gown to expose my thighs and straddled his
lap. He pulled the straps to my night gown away
from my left shoulders. When his lips touched
my flesh it was like fire. The heat sent waves
through out my body. His hands caressed my back
as his mouth found my breast. My body scream
out as he caressed it. We were both oblivous to
any other thoughts at that moment. My goal was
to only feel what was happening at that moment.
I didn't want to think about nothing and no one
but Harry. I could hear myself saying his name.
Oh Harry, I said as his mouth moved over my
breast and on up my neck to my mouth. I could
feel his hands on my butt cheeks pulling me

closer to him. Then he pulled the strapes to my gown completely down and both breast were exposed. He had to give me some kind of release. He knew intercourse was out of the question because he promised my father. But he also knew that I had to do this right now. He scooted to the edge of the sofa and buried his face into my breast. I was almost to the point of an orgasm. He didn't want to do anything to kill the moment so he let my body do all it needed to. As I released he held me close. He turned to lay back on the sofa and allowed me to lay on top of him. Are you ok, he asked. Yes I answered as I tried to slow my breathing. I was wondering why we didn't have intercourse but I didn't want to ruin the moment with questions. I guess I was too quiet and he knew that I had something on my mind. I'd like to keep my promises he said. What are you talking about?

I made a promise to your father. Oh, that I

said. Yes that, and I plan to keep it until

after we are married. I hope you can handle the

next two days Harry Stonewell, cause I won't

make it easy for you. We both laughed. I

decided to discuss all my fears with him. Harry

I think I know whats bothers me the most. What

is that sweetness. Remember when we stayed with

the baby the first night? Yes. I was on my

back when we were on the floor. Right, he said.

I think I am having problems with that. I mean

being on my back and being with you. Well,

would you like to do a little experiment? What

kind of experiment, I asked? Come with me. We

were up and off the sofa and headed to the

bedroom. Harry pulled the covers back and asked

me to get in and I did. He got in behind me and

said lay on your back. He laid down beside me.
Now, what are you feeling? I don't know, I
guess nothing. Good. He then put his leg
across mine. Does this bother you? No. Harry
then put his arm across my waist. How about
now? I feel a little uncomfortable. But it is
not bad. Harry got up on his knees and leaned
over me. What about now? Harry what is this
proving? Just an experiment now tell me how you
are feeling. He leaned his head down and began
kissing me on the shoulders. Not bad, I said.
He made his way to my breast and then down my
stomach. Not bad at all, I said. Does it
bother you for me to be right here, he said as
he kissed my right thigh. Oh no, not at all, I
yielded to the feelings that stirred up inside
of me. He rubbed his hand over her stomach and
brought it down between my legs. He waited for

a reaction from me. I was amazed at the
intenseness of what my body needed. He climbed
back up in the bed with me. You see sweetie,
it will be alright. Your body knows what it
needs and who it needs. So relax and enjoy your
body. He continued to caress me and I did enjoy
my body over and over again.

I woke up the next morning wrapped in
Harry's arms. It was a good feeling. I don't
remember getting undressed during the night but
my night gown was no where to be found. As he
slept I took the opportunity to explore his
body. I ran my hand over his chest and down his
stomach. I willed my mind to not think but to
just feel. I ran my hand over the top of his
pajama pants and I could feel that he had an
erection. Was he dreaming about me? I smiled.
I continued to touch him and he began to move.

I wanted to feel him in my hand. I eased my
hand down the top of his pj's and came in
contact with his tool.   As I messaged him he
woke up staring at me. Good morning, I said.
Good morning to you too. What a way to wake up
he said. I was curious an dedide to see what I
was missing. Be careful woman, you are flirting
with trouble. Is that right? I was already
turned on when I began my exploration of his
body. So he didn't have much work to do. I had
made up my mind that we would take this further
this morning. Harry turned onto his side pulled
me closer to him. We both had morning breath
but we were so into the moment to care. He
kissed me as his hands roamed my body. He
placed his knee between my legs. The pressure
there only intensified. My hands were tugging
at his pants. Maria we shouldn't do this. No,

Harry I said as my lips found his again. No,
let me do this please. He pulled his pj's off
and threw them out of the bed. Now there was
nothing between us, he said. I ran my hand over
his butt cheeks and he finally realized that I
was serious about making love to him. He moved
his mouth down my chest to my breast. I was so
worked up that I almost begged him to make love
to me. You sure about this he whispered? I
captured his mouth with mine and climbed on top
of him. I felt like I needed to be in control
and not him. If I could get through the moment
of penetration, I was home free. We were locked
into a deep kiss as I lowered myself down on his
penis. He was so attentive, but so in need of
me as well. Tell me if I'm hurting you, he
said. I just sat there for a moment and he was
still. I began to move and we both saw that

everything was good. It was beautiful and it was everything Harry had said. It was not sex, we made passionate love. I had no thoughts of Malik, or Kentrel. It was just the two of us, and no ghost. He let me take charge and I not only enjoyed my body but his as well. He stroked me senually not sexually. I can't ever remember feeling this good. As we caressed each others body, I saw the love I was always looking for. The look my father gives my mother and the look she returns to him. I understand those silent looks now. I have them for Harry. He made me feel so complete and now I feel like a real woman. While my thoughts were all over the place he was working up an orgasm that took us both by storm. We were lost into mindlessness. I had not even realized that I was in the position that I feared for so long. A man on

top of me. As I opened my eyes and saw Harry's
face, I did not have fear. I felt love, love
for the man I was going to marry in two days.
We both climaxed at the same time and both were
satisfied beyond degree. Harry continued to
rest on top of me and I allowed him to remain
there. Are you ok, he asked? I am so good you
might not get this smile off my face today.
Just don't wear it around your father. Look, I
know you made a promise to him, but this is
something that we needed to do. We might have
been crazy by Saturday. We both laughed. Come
on I'll give you a shower, he said. Sounds good
to me. We showered and dressed and went out for
breakfast.

CHAPTER TWENTY-FOUR

We finally made it to Mrs. Sara's to pick up the baby. I was wondering what was keeping you two. Did you forget that I have to pick up my dress this morning? We are so sorry Mrs. Sara, I said. Honey when are you going to stop calling me Mrs. Sara? Mom will do. Thank's mom. Would you like us to take you, Harry asked. No, I have a few more errands to run while I'm out. Ok, well we will be going then. Thanks for keeping Kaitee for us. It is no problem, she is such a sweet baby. Sounds like granny had a good time with her grand-daughter, I said. Yes we did and we can't wait till the next time, Mrs. Sara replied. Soon Mom, Harry said. Who is going to have Kaitee during the wedding, Mrs. Sara asked? We never thought about it, I said. Well, she can stay in the room with me until you and mama walk in and then she can sit with one of you. All right, then we will just have to have someone walk her in to you Mom. I would be more than happy to have her sit with me, Mrs. Sara said. Good then that is settled. What time is it, I asked? It's 10:15. Ok, we need to be going. I need to pick up my dress and Kaitee's dress. Where are you getting dressed, Harry said and how are you getting to the church? The girls and I are getting dressed at my place and the limo is picking us up there also. What about you and the guys Harry? Eddie is picking me up. Good everyone knows where they are supposed to be. Now lets get these dresses and then we can go home. When they were in the car, I asked him if he would stay at his apartment tonight and the night before the wedding. What's wrong, he asked? Nothing. The

girls are all coming over and Gayle is going to
stay the night before the wedding to help me out
and we are having a lady's night out tonight.
That's not a problem but I will be tossing and
turning in my bed tonight. Why? I'll be
looking for you. I smiled. It won't be long.
Oh before I forget, I have spoken with a
realitor and there are a few houses we need to
look at. Do you want to go and see them today.
Let's do this after the wedding. I don't think
we will have time, but if you have the time to
go then do it and you can tell me about it.
Bring some pictures back if you can. Ok, I will
do that.

Harry met up with the guys and they had a
bachelor party already planned for him. So did
the girls for me. Their little girls night out
turned into a big party at the Roxton with a

male stripper and just about every one I knew.

As the stripper danced around me I could only

think of my Harry. His strong chest, capable

arms and masculine hands. When my body quivered

at the thought of him touching me again. I

smiled and accepted his dance for what it was.

I was slightly embarassed when he came up to me

shaking himself all in front of me. I turned my

head away and he went on to the other ladies in

the room. Gayle notice the expression on my

face and decided to cut it short. She grabbed

the mike and thanked him for his time. I was so

grateful as I mouthed the words "thank you" to

her. She smiled and mouthed "no problem" back

to me. The evening was good and we had a great

time. Gayle and I made it back to the apartment

about 1:30 in the morning.

Harry's party was similar to mine. The guys

had the stripper and everything. He was not
amused and allowed his friends to enjoy them
selves. His mind was on me and wondered if
everything was going all right with me. He was
glad when it was over and headed home around
12:30. He was waiting for us to drive up. He
pulled out his cell phone and dialed my cell
phone. Hi, he said as he stepped outside his
apartment building. Did you have a good time?
Yes, what about you? It was ok, I just miss
being with you. Same here, hold on let me give
Gayle the key. I'm almost to your car hang up
the phone, he said. Hi Gayle he said. Hi
Harry, she said. He had his eyes glued to me
and Gayle knew she needed to disappear. Good
night Harry. Good night Gayle. Harry walked up
to me and captured my lips with his mouth.
Without touching me with his hands he had

managed to push some major buttons. He had

turned me on and all he used was his lips.

Gayle turned to look back and we were engaged in

a deep kiss. She had noticed the smile on my

face earlier when she picked me up. She

questioned me but I pretended that I didn't know

what she was talking about. I know she will

give me the third degree when we are a lone. As

he released my lips he took a deep breath. I

have wanted to do that all evening. I think we

had better take this inside, I told him. No, I

am going to leave you ladies for the night.

Lock up good and I will see you later today. I

love you sweetness. I love you handsome. He

waited till I was inside and I waved at him. He

disappeared and I turned to see Gayle watching

me. You two are like high school kids. I

laughed at her. We took turns in the shower and

then we laid across my bed and talked. Oh
Gayle, he is so wonderful to me. Let me tell
you what he did for me on Wednesday evening.
What girl? He made arrangements for his mom to
keep Kaitee. He met me here at the apartment
with flowers and told me that we were going out
to dinner. When I opened the door to the
apartment, he had a table in the center of the
living room. It had two long stem candles and
champagne chilling. What, Gayle said in
amazement? He poured champagne and then he
turned on the music. Gayle we danced and let me
tell you, he brought out some feelings in me I
had not felt in so long. It was a beautiful
evening. Then someone rang the doorbell and you
would never in a million years guess this.
What, tell me who was it, she said in a panic?
He had dnner delivered on covered trays. Gayle

it was an evening right out of a fairy tale. We
talked and danced and girl later on that night,
I have to tell you. Making love with Harry was
magical and yes it was definitely the most
sensual experience in my entire life. I thought
I knew pleasure Gayle, but until last night, I
didn't know anything. Gayle was in awe of her
friends attitude. I can't get over you. I am
so happy that you can experience the joy of love
making again. I held back on our conversations
about me and Ron because of the what happened.
You can say it Gayle. The rape, it's all right
to say it around me. Gayle was truly in awe of
the new Maria. I am so proud of you girl, she
said. Harry has brought so much to my life, I
don't know what to expect next. I am so
thankful for him. I just hope whatever this
surprise is that I don't break down and cry like

a baby. Yes, you and the rest of us. He is
such a romantic, I am definitely going to tell
Ron to take notes. We had better get to sleep
before we won't be able to get up in the
morning. What are we doing in the morning, I
asked? I don't know, just taking it easy I
guess and preparing for the rehearsal dinner.
Oh yeah. Good night Gayle. Good night Maria.

Day light came so quickly and we were both
so tired from staying out late and going to bed
even later. The phone rang and disturbed us
from sleep. I answered it but bearly awake. It
was Harry. Good morning baby, you still asleep?
Yeah, we were up pretty late last night. What's
up baby, I said? Gayle was also awaken by the
phone, but she did not let Maria know she was
awake. I missed waking up to you this morning,
he said. I missed falling asleep in your arms.

Gayle smiled as she listened to her friend.
Well, I wanted to take the two of you to
breakfast at Derbies but it's getting late.
What time is it? It's almost nine. All right
let me get Gayle up and we will be ready
shortly. I'm awake Gayle said as I hung up the
phone. What's going on? Breakfast in less that
twenty minutes. Oh my goodness, she said as she
looked at the clock. We really did sleep in
didn't we. You can go first and I will find
something to put on. I opened the door and
walked into the closet. I couldn't help but
feel a little sentimental. There hung my
wedding dress. Beautiful and perfect in every
way. I heard Gayle saying something as she came
out of the bathroom. Where are we going for
breakfast? Derbies. Ron's office is near by,
I'll see if he can join us. Great, I said as I

wiped the moisture from my eyes and pulled a
dress from the wall. Gayle was opening her bag
and pulled a dress out the same color but a
different style. We both just laughed. Gayle
picked up the phone and dialed Ron. He had just
gotten out of a meeting and was headed back to
the office. Yes, I can meet you all there, he
said. Good, I said as I exited the bathroom.
This will be a light makeup day cause I am not
feelin it. Harry was walking through the door.
Good morning ladies, it's me. Are you ready to
go? Gayle was putting on her shoes and I opened
the bedroom door. Harry was so eager to wrap
his arms around me. Hi baby, I said as our lips
touched. It is good now he said. He was
dressed in a pair of blue jeans and a polo
shirt. He smelled so good. What's with the
twin thing he said? We both laughed. I had no

idea Gayle had brought that color to put on,
honest it just happened. He shook his head.
Well you both look absolutely gorgeous. Thank
you and I must say Harry you are looking quite
scrumpteous yourself. Thank you Gayle. Oh Ron
is meeting us, I hope you don't mine me inviting
him? Not at all, it will be nice to finally
meet him. Harry did you check on Kaitee? No we
can call from the car.

Breakfast was good and we all made a point
to definitely do it again really soon. Ron was
delighted to meet Harry and they clicked. Ron's
office called and he needed to leave. We all
had places we needed to be, so we finished up
our breakfast and were on our way. Mama was
waiting on us to help out with the food for the
rehearsal dinner. Harry needed to pick up
Kaitee from his mothers and then we would rest

until the rehearsal. Time was definitley winding down.

The food was finished and so were we about 4:30 that evening. I was exhusted along with everyone else. Gayle and I went to the apartment to try to catch a nap and then shower and change for the rehearsal. We set the clock for an hour and layed our heads down. The clock went off and I could not belive that it had been a hour since we closed our eyes. I rushed and showered and changed, then Gayle. We arrived at the church and were the first to arrive. I should have known every one wouldn't be on time, I said. Don't get all worked up girlfriend. People are getting off work and will be pulling in soon. She was right. Mama, Daddy, Angel, Harry and Kaitee all walked in. They were followed by Harry's groomsmen and my bridemaids.

Jarell the organist, Penny and Curtis who are going to sing all walked in and Pastor Martin came in from the back of the church. Everyone spoke and were waiting on me. I guess everyone is here. I walked over and spoke to Jarell who then began to play the soft music we had chosen for them to come in on. Get use to this song bridemaids and groomsmen. This is your music. Just then my two ushers Alonzo and Garret walked in. Good to see you guys. I motioned for Jarell and Penny got his attention to stop playing. These are the ushers, they need to know what music to listen for to bring in the mother of the groom and mother of the bride. When this song is played you are to be walking in Harry's mother. I need some one to stand in for Harry's mother please. I showed Garrett how to hold her arm and escort her to the first pew

on the right side of the church. You will then
do a polite bow to her and walk away toward the
wall and come all the way to the back. Alonzo
you will bring your Aunt Audrey in when Garrett
comes back and the wooden gates are closed. You
will do the same thing Alonzo, once she has
taken her seat, you will bow politely and walk
towards the left side of the wall and return to
the back. When Alonzo comes through the gate
and it closes the music will change. It will
then be time for the ladies to come through.
Gayle will show you the pace. Gayle walked down
the isle at a nice easy pace not too slow and
not to fast. If you pay attention to the music
you will be able to walk with the beat. When
you reach the burgundy bow on the pew, you will
wait for your escort to come and get you. Eddie
would you please come for Gayle. Also Eddie

will have your flower.   Eddie pretend you are

holding a long stem red rose. Harry was amazed

at what he was hearing and how well she was

handling the job of being the bride and the

coordinator. You all have to remember there

will be no one out here telling you what to do.

It is so important that you know what to listen

for and where you are to be.   Penny remembered

that Antionette had a some plastic long stem

roses in her office. She asked Pastor Martin if

we could use four of them and he went to get the

for us. He returned and gave each of the

groomsmen one. Thank you Pastor Martin I said.

I walked over to the guys and I had a little

talk with them. Now guys I don't know all of

you well enough to know if you are married or

have girlfriends. But when you are walking with

that flower I want you to imagine that you are

taking it to the woman that you are madly in love with. I want you to be real about it. I promise I won't get you into any trouble. They all laughed. I returned to the bridemaids. Now ladies these guys are going to be charming you as they walk up to you and I want you all to put on that giddy smile you get when you see you man coming towards you. I am looking for the puppy love look. I want to see that when I watch my video. They all laughed. Now every one take you places. I walked over towards the middle of the church. Jarell started the music and Joni was first. She nailed the walk to the burgundy bow and waited for Andrew to come for her. He held the flower with both hands and strolled towards her. She smiled as he moved in closer to her. This is what I am looking for, did you see how he presented the rose to her. She

waited a second and then she took it and he
escort her to the right side of the room. Now
Andrew, I want you to stand off a half of a step
to the back of her. Perfect. Did you guys see
that? They all said yes. Mr. and Mrs. Dolace
were amazed at their daughter. They had no idea
she even knew what she was doing. Evidently she
had planed her wedding a long time ago. Porcha
was next. She swayed down the isle to the beat
of the music and Melvin came to escort her. He
was so cool. He let the rose dangle down by his
side as he strolled towards her. He stood
before her and reached for her hand. When she
gave it to him, he placed the flower in it. He
then took her by the arm and escorted her down
the isle. He positioned himself just as Andrew
did with Joni. I was almost in tears as I
watched them. Now it was Carlan's turn. She is

my beauty queen cousin. She should have been named elegance, cause that's what she is. She moved down the isle so gracefully. Kendrick must have fallen in love looking at her because he was so real with his movement. He moved as graceful as she did. He positioned the rose behind his back and walked slowly towards her as to make her wait for him to get there. She was charmed by his demeanor. He tilted his head and looked at her. Then he removed the rose from behind him and held it in his hands. He looked at it and then at her. Then he offered it to her. Everyone in the church were grinning from ear to ear. She took a deep breath and received his rose. He then kissed her hand and escorted her down the isle to the left in front of Joni and Andrew. Harry finally called out to Eddie. Eddie you got your work cut out for you man.

Being that Gayle and Eddie had already been

through the routine, I decided to not watch them

and have a talk with my little sister.

I called her to the back with me. Hi

sweetie. You ready to do me a huge favor? She

was grinning from ear to ear. You are going to

walk down the isle on this white plastic paper

ok. Ok, she said. Now you will have a basket

filled with pretty flower petals. You are going

to drop them on the floor all the way down to

the front. Ok she said shaking her head. Now

when you get to the front. There will be some

bells on the floor by the last pew. You are

going to put you basket down and pick up the

bells. Then I want you to turn around and go

back down the isles ringing the bells and shout

as loud as you can. Get up everybody the bride

is coming. Angel was laughing so loud that

everyone turned around to see what was going on.
Now here is your basket and you will pretend
that you are dropping the flowers and don't
forget the bells. I will be standing right here
with Daddy watching you when you go down the
isle ok. Jarell played more soft music as Angel
did what I told her to do. She made it to the
last pew and she put down the basket beside the
bells and picked them up. She turned around and
shouted really loud " Get up everybody the bride
is coming, the bride is coming". Mrs. Dolace
had a smile on her face that could have lit up
the room. The doors are going to open Daddy and
you and I will walk down the isle together. Ok
princess. Now I am going down there and wait
for you. I hurried down the isle and waited
inside one of the pews for my Daddy. Once we
get to the last pew Daddy, Harry will come for

me. Eddie's girlfriend was here with him. I
asked him what her name was and he said Kelsye.
I called her to stand in my place. She came up
and stood there for me. Harry you will come up
and shake my Daddy's hand and then Daddy you
will take a step back. Then it's my turn to
show you my walk, Harry said? No, stop
clowning. Then you take my hand and we step up
to Pastor Martin. Now Pastor Martin will tell
us what is next. Ok, I will began with….. He
went according to the program that I handed him.
Finally after Pastor finished he went back to
his office to wait for us to finish up. Jarell
wanted me to hear the songs. I took a seat
beside my mother to listen to the songs. Kaitee
was reaching for me and calling mama, mama,
mama. I took her in my arms and snuggled with
her for a few minutes. I knew she was missing

me as much as I had been missing her. She was learning how to walk so her feet were always busy. But right now she want mama and that just happened to be me. Harry smiled as he watched us. Once the song was finished, Jarell asked me if I needed to hear the other song. I told him that I was pretty comfortable with everything. Is everyone comfortable with what they are doing? Everyone said yes. Well, I know you are hungry and so am I, so lets eat.

We all walked over to the church hall. The aroma was wonderful. Aunt Maura and a few ladies from church were serving the food. Kaitee was hungry as well and I was holding her and digging in her sack at the same time looking for the baby food. My mother saw me struggling. Maria what are you doing? I'm looking for the baby food. Give me that baby. Kaitee's been eating table food for weeks now. She went into the kitchen and got the bowl she had prepared for her. No one told me they stopped giving her jarred food. Harry saw that I was stressed and he came over to get me. Baby let go of the tention right now. Harry, no one told me... Maria, shhh. He wrapped his arms around me and I held on to his waist. He kissed me and I had to remind him of where we were. Maria, I am not ashamed to show my affection or love for you anywhere. Tomorrow you will be my wife, my lover, and my friend. I don't ever want you to be ashamed of being affectionate with me. He was holding my chin while he spoke. He kissed me again and hugged me tightly. Come on let's get something to eat. We walked over to the window and picked up a plate. He carried both plates and I picked up the punch. Harry sat the plates on the table and then he took the drinks from my hands. He then pulled out my seat. When I sat down I could feel eyes on me. I looked up and everyone was watching us. It is awesome to see how people react to someone treating a woman with respect. But we ignored them and began eatting our meal. Gayle sat down beside me with her plate. Maria you have it all together. I think it is going to be wonderful. I can't wait until tomorrow, she said. Everyone finished their meals and were getting up to leave. Gayle stood up and made sure that everyone knew that they had to be here at the church for 5:15. We all were preparing to leave when I walked to the kitchen to thank the ladies for helping and give Aunt Maura a big hug. Once I finished up I meet Harry in the hallway. He had already picked up Kaitee from Mrs. Dolace.

Are you ready to go Gayle interrupted. Yes, I
am. Harry I can keep Kaitee tonight. No way,
Kaitee is staying with Granny Sara tonight. How
will she get dressed. Granny will dress her. I
will stop by and pick up her things. You need
to get your sleep and be ready to get your hair
and nails done in the morning. Remember, Ginger
and Zoe will be by around 9:15. So go home and
get ready for bed. I will give you a wakeup
call in the morning. Ok you two, Gayle said.
Let's say good night and we can go home. Harry
held on to my face as we kissed good night. The
ride home was so relaxing. I was so ready to go
to sleep. Tomorrow was going to be a busy day.
Gayle and I were in bed and conversation was out
of the question. We were both exhausted.

CHAPTER THIRTY-FIVE

The phone rang just as Harry promised. It was 8:00 in the morning. I am bringing your breakfast so don't come out until I am gone. I heard the noise in the living room. Harry had a table put up and the same caterer who brought our dinner that night was the same one who brought me breakfast. Gayle, you have got to see this. We both got up and put on our robes and slippers. Harry called and told me it was safe to come out. Gayle and I walked into the living room. Good morning madam the waiter said. He pulled out the chair for me and then Gayle. Another man brought in the trays. One held the tray and the other served the food from it. It was so romantic and so good. The man handed me a phone. Hello sweetness. Hi baby. Happy wedding day. Thank you Harry. Happy wedding day baby. I love you. I love you too sweetness. See you at the alter. Bye Harry. Girlfriend, Ron had better take some notes from this man. I am so touched. I smiled and shrugged my shoulders. We finished our breakfast. The hair dresser showed up and did our hair and nails. Once our nails dried it was time for lunch and of course before we could order lunch, the caterer returned and we sat down for lunch. Harry phoned again and we spoke briefly. I wish I could hug you right now Harry. I can't wait to see you either sweetness. But these guys won't let me out of their sight, he said. I might run down the isle to get you. We both laughed. Well, my beautiful bride, I will see you in a few hours.

It was 4:00 and it was time to get dressed. Gayle got dressed first and then she assisted me

with my dress. Mama, Daddy and Angel showed up
and Gayle let them in. Every one looked so
gorgeous. I stepped out of my room and they all
stared at me. Oh Henry look at her. Sister you
look beautiful. My hair was pulled back but
hanging in the back. The limo pulled up outside
and the driver rang the doorbell. Daddy told
him we would be ready in a minute. Joni, Porcha
and Carlan were all dropped off and we were
finally ready to leave. It was ten minutets to
five. I handed Gayle Harry's ring. She was
shocked. Maria this is awesome. Daddy drove
his car and the rest of us climbed into the
limo.

The church was decorated beautifully by the
florist. The florist used roses and babies
breathe for the décor. The candles in the choir
stand were waiting to be lit by Alonzo and

Garret. The church was filled to capacity by five fortyfive. We waited in one of the classrooms in the front. Mrs. Sara and Kaitee arrived and she was tugging to get to me. Baby, your mama needs to stay pretty and you will drool all over her beautiful gown, Mrs. Sara told her. Mrs. Sara, I mean mom, give her to me. This is one of those momets when wisdom prevails over common sense, I said. She can't understand anything but what she wants. She was so cute in her little dress with all the lace and satin. Hello sweetheart. Did you miss me? Kaitee held me tightly around the neck. Mumma, Mumma she mummbled until she was satisfied and then she went back to Mrs. Sara. The guys all had their flower the the maid they are going to escort. Harry and Daddy their boutineires. I had my bouquet made of mauve and burgundy roses with pearls that accented the roses. I wore diamond stud earrings and a beautiful thin diamond braclet that my father gave me for my last birthday. This was my something old. The earrings were borrowed for my mother and my garter was blue. The something new, well my dress is definitely new and I will leave it at that. Garret knocked on the door and Gayle answered. It's time he said. Everyone turned to me. You ready girl? Yes I'm ready. Mrs. Sara and my Mama walked out of the room along with the bridemaids. Gayle stayed behind with me and Angel and Kaitee. Alonzo and Garret did a wonderful job escorting both mothers. Once they Alonzo came back he carried Kaitee down the isle to Mrs. Sara. Jarell ended the music for the mothers and begin the music for the bridemaids. Everyone did just as they had done

last night at rehearsal. Everyone loved how the
groomsmen came for their maids. It was
priceless. Finally it was time for Angel to do
her thing. She was adorable. When she put down
her basket and picked up the bells and turned to
the crowd, I thought she might get a little
stage fright. But she was unbelievable. She
yelled as loud as she could. "Get up everybody,
the bride is coming". They all stood up,
laughed and applauded as the doors opened and
Daddy and I stood in the doorway. The music
began to play and I could feel my knees getting
week. My Daddy felt it too. He leaned over to
me and kiss me on the cheek. Princess keep your
eyes on Harry. There he was, my knight in white
shinning armor. Looking like he steped off the
cover of a magazine. My man, my husband, my
lover, and my friend. The music began and I

took a deep breath. Daddy and I were on our way. I heard the guest as they whispered how beautiful I looked. Yes, I looked grand. But, it wasn't for them, it was for me. I focused my attention back to Harry and I smiled at how the right corner of his mouth curled up when he smiled at me. Daddy and I made it to the last pew. He turned to me and lifted the viel as I had instructed him to do. He hugged me tightly and kissed me again on the cheek. I love you Daddy. I love you too princess. Harry was standing before us. He and Daddy hugged each other and shook hands. Then he turned his attention to me. The look in his eyes was pure love. No one could mistake it for anything else. He reached for my hand and we moved forward to stand in front of Pastor Martin. He smiled at the two of us and nodded as to signal he was ready to begin. "Dearly beloved, we are gathered here in the sight of God and these witnesses…". I could feel the flutters in my stomach. Then I could hear my Daddy as we were standing in the doorway to come in. "Keep your eyes on Harry". I looked at Harry and he smiled at me. God knows my feelings wasn't about whether or not I was doing the right thing. It was about how lucky I was feeling at that moment. I have so many people that love me in this church. I have an abundance of family, friends and co-workers that surrounded me on this day, my wedding day. And yes, God gave me Harry. I could hear Pastor Martin say "who gives this woman to be married to this man"? My Daddy proudly stepped forward and said "her mother and I do". Pastor Martin said to us "turn and face each other". I felt like the giddy school girl as I looked into his eyes.

When Pastor Martin asked Harry "Harry Cade

Stonewell, do you by God and the laws of this

state take Maria to be your wife" Yes, I do, he

said with so much emotion that the entire

congregation laughed. Maria Anielle Dolace, do

you by God and the laws of this state take Harry

to be your Husband? I do, I replied. Pastor

continued and we both repeated our vows to each

other. Then there was the exchanging of rings.

Eddie handed Harry the ring for me and Pastor

Martin asked him to repeat after him and he did.

He placed the ring on my finger. He then turned

to me. Gayle handed me the ring for Harry.

Pastor had me to repeat after him and I did the

same by placing the ring on Harry's finger.

After Pastor prayed, Penny and Curtis sang the

Lords' Prayer. We signed the license along with

the rest of the wedding party. My mother and Mrs. Sara lit the two unity candles and Harry and I followed them and lit the middle candle together and blew out the two separate candles. Penny read the meaning of the unity candle while it was all taking place. We returned to the front of the church and someone had placed a beautifully covered stool type seat at the alter. Eddie had replace Jarell at the organ and Andrew was standing beside Eddie with a guitar over his shoulder. Harry escorted me to the seat as Curtis handed him the microphone. Eddie and Andrew began to play. Harry walked out in front of me. I am so glad he gave me a seat, because the moment he opened his mouth and began singing I had goose bumps. He was smooth and yes oh so sexy. He sang the song "Flesh of my Flesh". When he kneeled down in front of me

and sang directly to my face, I cried. He was
prepared for my tears. He pulled a handkerchief
from his coat and handed it to me and never
stopped singing. He had just about every woman
in the church with tears in their eyes. If you
didn't feel the love you just didn't have a
heart. When he ended the song he reached for my
hand and kissed it as he whispered so softly, "I
love you Maria. If you weren't crying before
believe me you probably couldn't help it after
that sentimental display. The guest were not
only clapping and wiping their eyes, they were
standing as well. Pastor Martin said Harry and
Maria by the power invested in me, I pronounce
you man and wife. You may now kiss your bride.
I stood up and Harry handed the microphone to
someone behind him. He kissed me for what
seemed like an eternity. It was actually less

than a minute but it felt like eternity. Pastor Martin then said, "I present to you, Dr. and Mrs. Harry Stonewell". We walked out of the church as if we were the only two people in the world. Since everyone had their rides, we headed striaght the limo. Harry made sure I was all the way in train and all. Then he went around to the other side and got in. Hello Mrs. Stonewell. Hello Mr. Stonewell. We were wrapped in each others arms as everyone came out of the church. Someone tapped on the window. It was Gayle and Ron. Congratulations they both said. We will see you at the reception. The photographer and Videographer were taking pictures and filming as we waited in the car. Once the bridal party was out and heading to their cars, we began our ride to the reception. Harry took care of the reception and I didn't have a clue as to what the place looked like. I

just want to look at you, Harry said. Harry I

will never forget this day as long as I live. I

have heard of people having perfect weddings but

this is, oh my God I can't even explain it. The

car pulled up to the reception hall. There was

a sign that said "Congratulations Harry and

Maria". You are too much Harry, I said. They

got out of the car and walked inside the

building. It was gorgeous. There was a path

left open for people to walk to a dance area.

The area for photos was too much for words. The

back-drop from the cover of the program. The

doves pulling the ribbon from a bouquet of

roses. Two columns toped with a beautiful

arrangement of flowers. Vines dangling down

from the columns. Oh Harry this is beautiful, I

said over and over again. The wedding party

entered and the guest waited in the Hall's
entrance area. The photographer took pictures
and the guest were allowed in. We greeted them
as they entered. After about 15 minutes passed
we walked over to our table and took a seat.
The food was prepared in the back and brought
out on plates. The tables were already set up
with silverware. The cake was so elegant.
Harry had out done himself again. Once we had
eatten our food, we had our first dance as man
and wife. Harry chose "All My Life" by K-Ci and
Jojo. It was wonderful. Then we cut our cake
and walked around to socialize a bit. I was so
tired when I made it back to my seat I just sat
there watching everyone. Gayle sat down beside
me. Well, how does it feel to be a married
woman? Tired. Come on tell me how you feel. I
did girl, I told you I'm tired. We both

laughed. Seriously Gayle, I am on top of the world. No one deserves to be happier Maria. I can't wait for your wedding Gayle. It will be awesome. Yes, now that I see what you can do in a pinch, you are going to help me plan my wedding. We both laughed as we sat and watch people dance. Harry and my father were into a conversation and Mama was holding Kaitee while talking to a few of our cousins. I hope she was not giving out too much of my business. Angel played with some of her cousins her own age and I could not believe who my eyes feel on next. Adrenna, Kentrel and Cedric. They walked up to where Gayle and I were sitting. Congratulations Maria, Kentrel said. Thank you, I replied. We wanted to come by and drop off our gift and congratulate you and your new husband. She already said thank you Kentrel. No Gayle it's all right. People change and you have to allow them to change. Isn't that right Adrenna. I stood up as I made the statement. Harry and my Daddy saw them walk in and was headed over to the table. Baby is everything all right, Harry asked? Yes, everything is fine. I would like for you all to meet my husband, Dr. Harry Stonewell. Harry you already know Adrenna and you have met Kentrel. This is Kentrels friend Cedric. They all reached out to shake his hand. It's a pleasure to meet you Dr. Stonewell Cedric said. Yes, we wanted to bring our gift and say congratulations Kentrel said again. Thank you all for your well wishes. Please stay and enjoy the evening with us. Thank you, they all said as they walked away to the bar that was set up on the other side of the room. Oh God, I need a drink, I said. No sweetness, you just need me.

Harry took me in his arms, pressing his lips to mine. May I have this dance, he said? Yes you may have all of my dances. Save one for your old man, my Daddy said. I scooped up my trian and my husband guided me to the dance floor. Harry knew that my favorite musician is Luther, so he had the band to play one of his songs. The band played "Here and Now". This was all so familiar for Kentrel. He knew that I love this song and watching me dance to it with another man, who is now my husband was more than he could handle. It wasn't long before he left. Harry spent the hold song singing in my ear and looking into my eyes. In my prayers this night I thanked God for Harry. I thanked him for all the bad things that happened in my life. I know it sounds strange. But, if it had not been for the bad things, I wouldn't know how good it

could really be and that's the way it is.

Author Bio

Sandra Lusk was born and raised in Baton Rouge, Louisiana. She is married and has one child. Sandra had a love for books and novels even as a child and on into adulthood. Seeing through the eyes of the characters in those novels inspired her to write.

Sandra wants the words of her stories to leap off the page and become real to the reader. She wants the readers to feel the love, passion, emotions and yes even the anger of the characters portrayed in her stories.